Powerful, prominent, proud—the Oklahoma Wentworths' greatest fortune was family. So when they discovered that pregnant mom-to-be Sabrina Jensen was carrying the newest Wentworth heir—and had vanished without a trace— they vowed to…Follow That Baby!

Michael Wentworth: For a guy who had everything, megarich Michael lacked the two things he needed most: a convenient bride and a one-way ticket out of Wentworth Oil Works. But when a very marriageable mom-to-be literally landed on his doorstep, would she agree to temporarily tie the knot?

Beth Masterson: After huffing and puffing in Lamaze class with the elusive Sabrina Jensen, Beth felt she owed the Wentworths news of the woman's last-known whereabouts. But when her good deed netted her a very good-looking husband—and a good-size case of love—she second-guessed her good intentions.…

Sabrina Jensen: Beth's tip placed the pregnant runaway's hideaway closer than ever. But would the Wentworths be the first on the scene…or would Sabrina's baby beat them to it?

* * * *

Don't miss
THE MERCENARY AND THE NEW MOM by Merline Lovelace, the exciting conclusion to Follow That Baby, available next month in Silhouette Intimate Moments.

Dear Reader,

The lure of the West is as strong today as it was a hundred years or more ago, when the wagon trains headed in that direction. I know I can't resist a cowboy. And when he's also a sheriff…! So is it any wonder that heroine Ginny Marlow finds herself inextricably entwined—and loving it!—with Quint Cutler? In *The Law and Ginny Marlow,* the latest in award-winner Marie Ferrarella's miniseries THE CUTLERS OF THE SHADY LADY RANCH, you'll see what happens when a quick trip out west turns into a lifetime of wide open spaces. You'll also be sorry there's only one more book to go in this wonderful family's story.

And if you've been following our cross-line miniseries FOLLOW THAT BABY—or even if you haven't—you've got a treat in store with Christie Ridgway's *The Millionaire and the Pregnant Pauper.* This homegrown Yours Truly star tells a romp of a tale—and takes you one book closer to the discovery of the missing Wentworth heir. Have a good time now, and next month travel to Silhouette Intimate Moments to see how the saga ends.

Have fun, and don't forget to come back next month for two more fun and fabulous books all about meeting—and marrying!—Mr. Right.

Yours,

Leslie J. Wainger
Executive Senior Editor

Please address questions and book requests to:
Silhouette Reader Service
U.S.: 3010 Walden Ave., P.O. Box 1325, Buffalo, NY 14269
Canadian: P.O. Box 609, Fort Erie, Ont. L2A 5X3

Christie Ridgway

THE *MILLIONAIRE* AND THE *PREGNANT PAUPER*

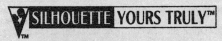

SILHOUETTE YOURS TRULY™

Published by Silhouette Books
America's Publisher of Contemporary Romance

For the little boys who call me "Mom" and "Aunt":
Bryan, Jesse, Taylor and Paxton.

SILHOUETTE BOOKS

ISBN 0-373-52084-0

THE MILLIONAIRE AND THE PREGNANT PAUPER

Copyright © 1999 by Harlequin Books S.A.

Special thanks and acknowledgment to Christie Ridgway for her contribution to the FOLLOW THAT BABY series.

Printed in U.S.A.

Dear Reader,

This is so exciting! I'm thrilled to be a part of the FOLLOW THAT BABY miniseries. The hero of *The Millionaire and the Pregnant Pauper*, Michael Wentworth, isn't quite as excited. While he's hoping the New Year will ring in some changes to his life, he can't imagine the drastic makeover that Beth Masterson will bring to him.

Can a millionaire playboy become a down-home family man for a lifetime? Beth sure hopes so!

As we begin to count down to the year 2000, I'm counting my blessings, as well. I'm wife to a wonderful, romantic man, mother of two sons, and busy volunteer at my boys' school. And thanks to you, I'm creating stories of love triumphant— what I know it to be.

I love to hear from readers. You may write to me at P.O. Box 3803, La Mesa, CA 91944.

All the best,

Christie Ridgway

Books by Christie Ridgway

Silhouette Yours Truly

The Wedding Date
Follow That Groom!
Have Baby, Will Marry
Ready, Set…Baby!
Big Bad Dad
The Millionaire and the Pregnant Pauper

1

The two-hundred-year-old grandfather clock in the foyer wheezed. Michael Wentworth burrowed deeper into the library's leather couch and counted each raspy gong...seven...eight...nine.

Hell. Three more hours until midnight.

New Year's Eve. A playboy's Night of the Year. Who would believe on tonight of all nights, instead of guzzling champagne and nuzzling beautiful women, he was counting clock chimes like Cinderella?

But that wasn't right. Cinderella possessed a healthy fear of midnight. Michael was more eager than a racehorse at final posting call for Baby New Year to show up on the doorstep.

Ding dang ding dong. Michael groaned. Not the clock this time, but the stuffy, stentorian tones of the front doorbell. "No one's home!" he yelled in the direction of the door.

With the staff off for the evening, he'd counted on being alone all night—except for his silent pals, Jack and Bud. Daniel's and Weiser, that is.

Ding dang ding dong. The damn doorbell again. Probably Elijah, with LeAnne or Val, pretending they'd never gotten his last-minute message that he wasn't going out tonight. "We've all gone away!" he yelled again, but got up and paced toward the door anyway. Neither he nor his friends were any good at taking no for an answer.

Unfastening one more button of his tuxedo shirt to make it absolutely clear he'd decided against the big bash at the Route 3 Club, Michael reached the entryway just as the annoying doorbell started up again.

"Keep your pants on, Elijah," Michael grumbled and pulled open the heavy wrought-iron-and-glass door.

But it wasn't Elijah on the other side. Not LeAnne or Val, either. It wasn't anyone he'd ever seen before. A waif stood before him, wearing jeans, a parka and a wide-eyed expression of shock.

"I'm Beth Masterson," the waif said in a breathy voice. Her hands tightened into fists and two white teeth clamped down on her lower lip. A moment passed, then she released a long breath. "I'm sorry to bother you, but I'm going to have a baby."

The bells and chimes had affected his hearing. "Pardon me?" Michael asked the waif. Only the dim beams of the foyer's sconces touched her—he hadn't bothered to turn on the outside lights—and her white-blond hair glowed like moonlight against her dark parka.

She shifted, and the ends of her hair swept over the blue nylon. "I'm—" she started again. Her hands recurled into fists and a visible shiver ran through her body.

"For God's sake—" Cupping her upper arms, he pulled her over the threshold, then shut the front door. The slick fabric of her coat felt cold beneath his palms, and he spun the nearby rheostat to add the illumination of the foyer chandelier.

She squinted against the blazing light and winced. Blue eyes. Lips nearly blue with cold, too.

"You didn't walk here, did you?" Michael glanced at her feet, sensibly covered in Oklahoma-winter boots. Had her car stranded her on the road?

She shook her head, as if her voice were gone, and went strangely still. After a moment the tenseness went out of her body. "Drove my car. Heater went out."

"And then you had to walk the length of the drive-way." Not sure what else to do with her, Michael gestured down the marble hallway toward the library where he'd been sitting. "I heard the buzz at the gate, but thought you were some, uh, friends, come to drag me out for the evening." It was a quarter mile of graveled path from the gate to the front door.

She didn't move, even though he waved in the direction of the library again. Michael shoved his hands in his trouser pockets. "Well, uh, is there something I can do for you, miss? A taxi? A tow truck?" One phone call and he could get back to his solitary New Year vigil.

Small, ringless hands crept over the parka toward her middle. "I'm really sorry, sir." She visibly swallowed, her neck muscles working against the frayed collar of the jacket. "But I told you a minute ago. I'm going to have a baby."

A dozen thoughts formed in Michael's mind, even as he ushered her to the closest seat in the foyer.

What was a young and ringless woman doing on the Wentworth doorstep?

She couldn't be the one pregnant with his late brother Jack's child. The Wentworth family was hunting for Sabrina Jensen. He'd seen her picture—had even met Sabrina's twin—and she looked nothing like this delicate waif.

She couldn't be a woman he'd dated then somehow forgotten. He *never* went without protection, and even on a hell-raising night he wouldn't forget that moonbeam hair.

So why—

Her fingers closed over his wrist. "I think—" Her voice stopped, and then grew strong like her grip on him, both reinforced by steel. "I need to get to the hospital *now*."

That galvanized him.

Terrified him, too.

But he'd watched enough mares give birth to know that you mostly tried staying out of a birthing mama's way. After a couple of Y-chromosome-induced bad suggestions—*no,* she did not want him to call the Wentworth family internist, and *no,* a Medivac helicopter wasn't necessary—she politely asked for a lift to the county hospital.

Oh, yeah, and they could even take her car.

He acknowledged that proposal with the nonanswer it deserved. Within minutes he made a quick call ahead to the hospital and bundled her into his truck. With the heat on full blast and the waif at semirecline on the passenger side, his sheepskin-lined coat thrown over her for extra warmth, Michael finally had a second to think through a few pressing particulars.

"I've got a cell phone right here," he said, darting a quick glance her way. "What's the number of the baby's daddy? I'll call him for you."

Her mouth tightened and then she tried a little smile. It wobbled a bit before she gave up. "It's 1-800-HE'S-GONE." She made a second valiant attempt at a smile. "But if you'd call Bea and Millie at the Freemont Springs Bakery and tell them I won't be in to work tomorrow…" Her voice trailed off and he knew another contraction had hit.

Michael tried talking to distract her. "Freemont Springs Bakery, huh? Well, I haven't had one of their rum cakes in too long. Do they still make those white cookies with the chocolate dot on top? My sister Josie loves their doughnut holes. And what about Millie's crullers? Now, she makes just about the best crullers—"

"You can stop now."

Michael glanced over again, and in the dashboard glow saw a sweet smile on her face this time, not a big smile, but a smile so real, so genuine, that—

That he couldn't wait to reach the county hospital that just this moment was looming on his right. This lady and her arriving baby and her smiles were nothing to him. Nothing beyond the Good Samaritan responsibility to get her to the delivery room on time.

He turned into the hospital driveway and followed the glowing arrows toward the emergency entrance.

Glancing over, he saw her white-knuckled fingers gripping the suede jacket across her legs. When she bit her bottom lip, his gut tightened.

What the hell could he do for her?

He found himself reaching over to pat her small fist.

Cold skin. He rubbed it gently until he braked at the emergency room entrance.

Shielding his eyes against the harsh lights, he jumped out of the parked truck. The hospital doors slid open and a staffer in scrubs quickly rolled out a wheelchair. "Baby?"

Michael nodded, but he somehow beat the chair to the passenger door and pulled it open. The waif turned toward him, and he drew her into his arms, then placed her gently into the waiting wheelchair. He stepped back. *Okay, she was somebody else's problem now.*

The chair rolled forward. "Wait!" he heard himself say, then he grabbed the suede-and-sheepskin coat and hunkered down in front of her to tuck it around her legs.

Her hand touched his shoulder.

Michael looked up.

The glare of the hospital lights washed the color from her face, but her hair gleamed like cold white fire and her eyes, blue, turquoise blue, unsettled him. "Thank you," she said and one cold finger touched his cheek. Then the wheelchair moved toward the entry and the double doors *whooshed* then *whooshed* again to swallow her up.

* * *

Whew. Michael stepped back into the truck and slammed the door shut behind him. Shoulders against the seat, he took a deep breath and tried to relax.

Couldn't.

The very air of the car smelled like the waif. A faint scent, though fresh and sweet. He cracked the window for a blast of Oklahoma cold, but that reminded him of the touch of her finger and the cool gleam of her moonlight hair.

Was she going to be all right?

He turned the ignition and goosed the gas pedal to drown the thought in the roar of eight shining cylinders. His plate had a full six courses already, without taking on anything more.

Curse Jack. Big brothers shouldn't die at thirty-five, especially not in a terrorist attack and explosion on an oil rig off the coast of Qatar.

Curse Grandfather. Bent on tracking down the particulars of Jack's death, Joseph Wentworth had headed for Washington D.C. Probably right now the old man was squelching every ounce of Christmas joy from any government official who hadn't been smart enough to head for Vail or Stowe over the holidays.

Curse Josie. Just for good measure Michael damned his newly married sister, too. The whole lot of them had allowed the family oil company's responsibilities to fall onto his shoulders.

Following Jack's death, Michael hadn't wanted any of it, but his grandfather, the old bastard, had a way of manipulating him. Just a few ominous rumblings from Joseph about "only a few years left" to his life followed by repetitions of "with Jack gone from the family now" made Michael beat a hasty retreat back to his oil company office before he did something stupid like sign a lifetime contract to run the place.

The hell of it was, everyone knew Joseph Wentworth had twenty-five good years left in him and they all belonged at the helm of Wentworth Oil Works. And if they never found the answer to Jack's death—or never found the baby he'd fathered before it—Joseph would need Wentworth Oil Works more than ever.

And Michael needed the hell out. With Jack dead, and their sister Josie wedded to rancher Max Carter, it was high time Michael got on with his own life— and his own dream. A man couldn't build a stable full of champion Oklahoma quarter horses from a penthouse office in the Wentworth Building.

Michael turned the truck in the direction of the hospital exit and glanced at the time. Nine-forty-five. At least it was closer to midnight. And midnight made it almost the new year, and in the new year he hoped to God that Grandfather would refocus on the family business instead of the family tragedy.

If only that elusive and pregnant Sabrina would show herself…

Pregnant.

The waif—Beth—popped into his mind again. And that wobbly smile of hers and the small fists she'd made to suppress her discomfort.

It was none of his business.

It was not his problem.

He belonged at home with a glass of whiskey in one hand and a longneck chaser in the other, watching Dick Clark and that damn apple fall.

Something other than his brain was in control, though. His foot stomped on the brake pedal, one hand jerked the car into reverse, back to drive, and then all ten fingers twisted the steering wheel to make the sharp left into the hospital's parking structure.

Some great mind at the Travis County Hospital had painted varicolored stripes on the floor that were supposed to lead visitors through the rat maze of corridors to their destination. On his way to maternity, Michael found the cafeteria four times and then the psychiatric wing.

Keep your head down, Michael instructed himself, his gaze darting away from the observant nurse-in-charge back to the rainbow-striped floor. He was crazy for following the waif into the hospital—no sense tempting fate to do something about it.

Walls painted with pastel storks told him he'd finally found the right place. A woman wearing a badge stood behind a desk. She raised her eyebrows and looked his way when he entered the deserted waiting area. Michael hurriedly found a seat and a *Sports Illustrated.*

"Waiting for somebody," he said to the lady. "I'll, uh, just be right here in case she needs something." Or until he came to his senses and went back home where he belonged.

Seconds later, a mouse of a woman in stork-printed scrubs rounded a corner and bellowed in Michael's direction. "There you are!" A militant fire burned in her eyes.

The fight-or-flight instinct popped him out of the chair. "What?" He tried that look-behind-him, look-beside-him, you-can't-mean-me move, but the mouse continued closing in.

She tucked a finger in the pocket of his tuxedo jacket and tugged him in the direction she'd come. "A man in a tux," she said in that earsplitting voice of hers. "They said she came in with a man in a tux."

Without stopping for breath, she pulled him around another corner to a carpeted corridor with wide doors on either side. Her voice fell suddenly to a whisper. "Sorry to interrupt your night, hon, but we're headed for a labor-and-delivery room where you're about to become a daddy."

Michael gulped. "But—"

"But nothing." With a whisk of her imaginary tail, Nurse Mouse had him out of the bright hall and into a dimly lit, soft-music-filled room.

"Beth, look who I found!" she called in a cheery voice to the woman on the bed.

The waif, looking warmer but as delicate as ever, didn't respond. Michael noted that her hands, lying against the blanket, tightened into fists. Another contraction. He wanted to move— ahead, away, somewhere—but the mouse had a firm grip on his arm.

A moment passed, then Beth's hands relaxed and her head turned his way. A strand of her impossibly white-blond hair stuck damply against her cheek.

He met her gaze and the back of Michael's neck burned. *What the hell was he doing here?* Though a gown and a blanket covered her completely, something about the hospital setting and the medical paraphernalia made him feel as if he'd stomped all over her modesty.

He smiled in apology. "I think I'd better—"

Nurse Mouse dug her tiny claws into his forearm. "I've got to check on another patient, young man. You're not going anywhere until I get back." The door clicked like a pair of angry heels behind her.

He smiled again at Beth and rolled his eyes in the direction of the door. "I think there's been a misunderstanding."

Her answering smile was that wobbly one he'd tried to forget. "Sorry. I think they assume…"

"Don't worry about it." He started backing toward the door. The waif was in good hands. Time to duck out of here and head back to his solitary New Year stakeout—what he should have done in the first place.

Shoving his fingers in his pockets, he continued backing away. "I'll just, uh—" His shoulders hit the door, and he pushed it open, ready to hightail it home.

Then that prehistoric kill-or-be-killed instinct kicked in again and he looked over his shoulder down the hall. Nurse Mouse's tiny strides were eating up the corridor carpet.

In his direction.

Michael stepped back in the room so quickly the

swinging door slammed him in the butt. "I think she's coming back."

"Oh dear—" But then Beth's expression tensed. Two lines dug themselves between her brows.

"Another one?" he asked unnecessarily.

Without thinking, he backed up again, his shoulders bumping the door. "I'll get the nurse." Somebody—anybody—instead of him should be here.

A barely perceptible shake of her head, but he caught it. He froze, his own hands tightening into fists as she rode the latest contraction.

Once she could breathe deeply again, so could he. "You okay?"

She nodded.

"Time for me to go then." It was. For Pete's sake, the poor woman probably craved some privacy.

She nodded again.

But before he could move he saw another contraction come over her. It started somewhere about her knees—even beneath the blanket he could see her legs stiffen—and then it moved to her shoulders, and then he found himself beside her, closer than he'd been when he'd lifted her from the car.

One of his hands enclosed one of her tight fists, and as her pain passed, the hand blossomed, its fingers relaxing into the warm hold of his.

He realized he was sitting on the edge of the bed. The back of his neck heated again as he watched a bead of sweat roll from her temple down to her chin. He didn't touch it, just watched it slide down the translucent skin of her face.

"Are you okay?" Once she reassured him, he'd

be able to leave her. "Tell me you're okay." He was whispering.

And so was she. "I don't want to admit this." She licked her dry lips. They were as colorless as her face and made the turquoise blaze of her eyes even more unsettling. "So don't tell anyone, will you? I'm just the tiniest bit scared."

No one left after that. People came in, though. More people. Lots of people. Some in stork stuff, the doctor in a long surgical-type robe, another someone wheeled in more equipment that Michael didn't want to know the use for.

At every new step he looked into Beth's eyes. He waited for her to ask him to go, but she didn't release him. Instead of making fists, she'd taken to riding through her labor with his hands as her lifeline and pretty soon he couldn't feel his fingers.

What the hey. Who needed fingers when a life was being born in this very room?

He kept his gaze on Beth's face. What was happening below her neck was between Beth and her doctor. What was happening between Michael and the waif was eye to eye. With his gaze, he tried telling her he believed in her, that he believed in her strength and in her female power.

And while her body brought a child into the world, Michael watched Beth transform from woman to mother—and felt as humbled by the event as a twenty-seven-year-old man in his prime could.

Finally, just after midnight, the room was silent, and nearly empty.

Most of the equipment was gone. But the bed was

there, and a clear plastic bassinet, and Michael, and Beth and this little red thing that looked like a peanut with arms and legs.

Beth's baby boy.

Snoozing, the infant lay against her chest. Beth's eyes were at half-mast, too. Michael had lost that eye-to-eye connection with her a while ago—the instant they'd placed her baby in her arms.

Something about the vision of woman and child brought a smile to his face. And something about that smile brought a welling surge of self-protective bachelor instinct. "I gotta get out of here," he said loudly.

He slapped his palms against his thighs and jumped from the chair he'd dragged beside the bed. It was high time he left. "Um, uh, congratulations."

She mumbled something sleepily.

Relieved, he started moving away. She was probably glad to get rid of him.

As it should be. His place wasn't beside her.

The door swung open and Nurse Mouse breezed into the room. "Don't go anywhere yet."

The commanding note in the nurse's voice set Michael's hackles rising again. "Look, I just gave this woman a ride to the hospital, okay? I'm not—"

"Wait a minute." Beth's eyes popped open and her head turned quickly toward him. She seemed to see him for the first time.

"Just one more thing." Nurse Mouse was beaming now. "Just one most exciting thing."

Smiling mouse nurses made Michael even more nervous than militant mouse nurses. She'd left the door to Beth's room open, and he saw a suspicious gathering of people there. "I don't have time for anything more," he protested.

"Wait a minute," Beth said again. She blinked, ignoring the fusses of Nurse Mouse who was adjusting her blanket and the baby's knit cap. "Wentworth, right? You *are* one of the Wentworths?"

He nodded, aware that the suspicious gathering was edging into the room. "We can talk about this some other—"

"Give me a second." One hand gently supporting the baby, Beth groped around and found the remote controls for the bed. With a little buzz, her head angled up. "I came to your house tonight to tell you something."

One of the smiling people approaching Beth's bed wasn't wearing a robe or scrubs and he was carrying a camera. A premonitory chill ran through Michael and a dying-fish queasiness began flopping around in his gut. "Some other time," he told Beth hastily. "I gotta—"

"Please. It's important."

Years of training halted Michael midhustle. He might be a wary bachelor, but he was a *gentlemanly* wary bachelor. Nurse Mouse used his good manners to push him back beside Beth's bed. "What is it?" he asked.

The man with the camera was aiming it at them. Nurse Mouse made a grand gesture in their direction. "This is the New Year's Baby," she announced. "The first baby born in Travis County this year!"

"Oh, hell," Michael muttered, suddenly knowing

where this was heading. He stepped out of the camera's range.

"I know where Sabrina is," Beth said.

"*What?*" Michael was so surprised, he stepped back toward her. "*Sabrina?*" A bulb flashed.

And that was how the front page of the *Freemont Springs Daily Post* came to look the way it did. Big headline: Freemont Springs Welcomes New Year's Baby! Big picture, too. Infant wearing T-shirt proclaiming Property of Travis County Hospital. New mama looking wan but happy. And in the daddy's place, stood Freemont Springs's most uncatchable bachelor. Yes, there was Michael Wentworth, staring straight ahead, eyes wide, mouth flies-welcome-here open to display as Dr. Mercer Manning, D.D.S., pointed out proudly and often, some of his very best dental work.

2

Joy radiated through Beth Masterson as she held her child against her breast. She touched her lips to the warm, downy head of her newborn son and peeked out the window at the morning sunlight. "A new year is a new beginning," she whispered to him.

Alice Dobson, the woman who raised Beth, had said those words every January first and probably still did. Though Beth had only exchanged a couple of letters with Alice since leaving the Thurston Home for Girls five years ago, she'd never forgotten the wisdom she'd learned from the older woman. "And I won't let you forget any of it, either," she said to her brand-new little boy. "Anything I've ever learned I'll pass along to you."

Which might not be saying a whole heck of a lot, she admitted to herself. In his sleep, her son's brow furrowed. She smiled, and tried smoothing out the wrinkles with a gentle fingertip. "Don't worry, baby. Mommy's getting smarter every day."

She sighed, wishing she'd been a little smarter months ago. Maybe then she'd have realized that Evan wasn't the kind of man to love her forever—if he ever had at all. "But then I wouldn't have you," she said out loud, tracing one tiny baby ear. Nothing would make her regret her son.

With just a few winces, she managed to slide off the bed and lay him in the clear isolette. She had more pressing things to wish for, anyway. With the baby's arrival almost a full month early, her savings account was a full month lighter than she'd hoped. And she should be wishing for a new—cheap— apartment to appear, too. Bea and Millie had rented her the room above the bakery only temporarily, and Millie's elderly mother was due to move there in four weeks.

Beth bit her lip. "But wishes don't wash dishes," she whispered to the baby. "Alice taught me that, too."

Determined not to surrender to her worries, Beth ran a hand through her tangled hair. A nurse had popped in a few minutes before and suggested she take a shower in the attached bathroom. A deluge of hot spray and she'd feel like a new woman.

A knock sounded on the door. Probably the nurse who'd promised to help her into the shower. "Come in."

The door opened and a man stepped into the room.

A flush burst over her skin and Beth clutched the thin fabric of her hospital gown. Oh, shoot. Had she wanted to feel like a new woman? Make that a completely *different* woman. Because the tall, dark and handsome near-stranger coming toward her had last night held her hand and shared the most intimate and miraculous moments of her life.

If only the mint-green-and-mauve hospital linoleum would develop a woman-size sinkhole right at her feet.

"Beth?" She remembered his voice, deep, like a man's should be. Slow too, like all Oklahoma voices were in comparison to the speedy Los Angeles chatter she was accustomed to.

He came three steps closer and held out his hand.

She reached across the baby's isolette to shake it. Memories welled up from the night before. His dark brown eyes serious, but speaking to her. Her fingers holding on to him as if she could wring strength from his hands. More embarrassment flooded her face with heat and she quickly broke their grasp.

"I'm Michael," he said, shoving his freed hand into the pocket of his jeans. "Michael Wentworth."

She hadn't forgotten. They'd sorted out his name last night, just after the reporter had snapped the New Year's Baby photo. Then Michael had disappeared. To be honest, she'd been so focused on her son since then that she hadn't given him much more thought.

Until this moment.

Now all she could think about was how he had seen her last night, how she must be looking this morning, how she wished she had taken that shower thirty minutes sooner....

How maybe she could nicely, politely, get rid of him *right this instant.*

Michael almost laughed out loud. Beth's expression was as readable as the front page headlines—God, squash that sore subject—let's just say he knew exactly what she was thinking.

She wanted him gone.

Well, too bad. The lady owed him an explanation and a few details. At the very least in repayment for that damn front page photo that had resulted in more pre-Wheaties phone calls than he'd ever received.

He smiled, the one he'd perfected in third grade Sunday school class. "I'll just take a few minutes of your time."

She gave him the same suspicious look that old Miss Walters had when he'd sworn he hadn't cribbed the day's Bible lesson. "I was just about to—" She made a vague gesture behind her and went back to twisting a bit of the hospital gown in her hands. "I really need to—"

"Answer just a few questions," he interjected smoothly. Someone had faxed his grandfather the front page of the *Freemont Springs Daily Post* this morning, and Michael's first phone call had been assuring Joseph that there wasn't *another* secret Wentworth heir. "I talked with my grandfather today and we're eager for your information on Sabrina."

Beth bit her lip. "Listen, um, I was in a really strange state yesterday. I cleaned out the trunk of my car. Then the glove compartment. I found thirty-seven cents between the cushions of the back seat. Next I started on my apartment."

Michael noted the color suffusing her face and found himself staring at her. Last night she'd been so pale. Moonbeam hair, pale complexion, colorless lips. But now a flush accented her delicate cheekbones. Her lips had reddened, too. The brightness took nothing away from the clear, beautiful color of her eyes.

Shaking himself, he realized she'd stopped speaking. "I'm sorry. You were saying? Thirty-seven cents?"

When she bit her lip again, the bottom part of her mouth went even rosier. "It's a pregnancy thing, you see. I read about it, but didn't even realize it was happening to me. I was nesting."

He raised his eyebrows.

"You know, getting everything ready. I had this compulsion to clean things, take care of loose ends. Two people I know have birthdays in March. Yesterday I had this undeniable urge to buy them cards and mail them."

None of this was getting him any closer to the Sabrina information. And, dammit, he didn't want to know any more about her. Not her March birthday friends, not her nesting urges, not the intriguing shape of her rosy mouth. "But about Sabrina—"

Three female hospital staffers entering the room shut him up. Two wore maternity nurse's scrubs, one a business suit. He looked at them in irritation, then realized he knew two of the three. "Hello, Deborah. Eve." He'd dated Deborah—the one in the suit—oh, two or so years ago. Eve had been his date last Halloween.

"Michael," Eve said, a curious expression on her face.

Deborah chimed in. "We thought we saw you come in here."

That dying-fish flip-flop started in his gut again. "I'm just talking with Ms. Masterson here."

"*Ms.* Masterson." Deborah giggled. "Ho ho. We saw that picture in the newspaper."

He suddenly remembered why he'd stopped dating Deborah. *Ho ho.* A glance at Beth showed she wasn't any more comfortable with the conversation than he was. "Did you come in to talk to me or the new mother?"

All three women looked embarrassed. Deborah spoke up. "I'm here to collect some hospital paperwork." She turned to Beth. "Is everything I gave you filled out?"

Michael ran his hands through his hair as Beth shuffled through some papers on the table beside the bed. *Get everybody out of here and get on with the questioning.* Being caught in Beth's room this morning was going to set the wheels of the Freemont Springs rumor mill turning.

As if they needed any help after this morning's photo.

Paperwork handed off, the three women headed back out the door. Michael didn't even wait until they were gone to get right to the point.

"What about Sabrina?" The sooner he got the information, the sooner he could get out of here and start recouping his bachelor reputation. "Listen, I promise I'll get out of your way if you'll just tell me what you know about her."

Beth leaned against the hospital bed. "I saw the photo and article about your search for her in a Tulsa newspaper last week. I wasn't sure exactly what to do...." She shrugged. "But last night I suddenly decided I *had* to tell what I know."

Michael held his breath. This could be the piece of information the family needed to find the mother of his brother's unborn child. "And?"

Beth hesitated, bit her lip, then squared her shoulders as if coming to a decision. "Sabrina is here in Freemont Springs. Or *was* here, anyway, until at least two weeks ago. We had some Lamaze classes together."

Here in town! "Thank you, Beth." A torrent of relief sluiced through him. "You don't know what this means to us—to my grandfather." God, if this could be the lead they needed! A grin broke over his face. "I could kiss you for this."

"And maybe for this, too," Deborah tittered as she peeked back around the half-open door.

The smile dying on his face, Michael swung to look at her.

"I'm just double-checking your son's birth certificate application, Ms. Masterson." Deborah rattled the papers she held. "Your handwriting is understandably a little shaky this morning."

Michael looked from Deborah back to Beth, whose face had suddenly turned crimson.

"It's M-I-C-H-A-E-L, Michael, correct?" Deborah continued, a little smile quirking the corners of her mouth. "You want to name your son *Michael* Freemont Masterson?"

Michael blindly punched the Down button on the elevator. Michael Freemont Masterson. He hadn't been able to get out of Beth's room fast enough after hearing that. *Michael* Freemont Masterson. She'd named her baby after *him.*

He waited for the anger or, at the very least, irritation to rise. When a bachelor was caught in the daddy spot for all the world to see, the last thing he wanted was for the baby to become his namesake. *Go ahead, Wentworth,* he told himself. *You have every right to be ticked off.*

The elevator doors slid open and Michael stepped into the hospital lobby. Between him and the doors to the parking structure sat a set of newsstands. *USA Today.* The *Wall Street Journal.* The *Freemont Springs Daily Post.*

His best friend Elijah Hill was buying the last copy.

Ah, hell.

"Michael, Michael, Michael."

Not even a second to hope Elijah wouldn't spot him. In jeans, cowboy hat and boots, Elijah was the picture of an Oklahoma rancher—exactly what he was.

"Shouldn't you be at home shoveling horse sh— manure?" Michael asked. If he didn't give Elijah an opening, maybe he could avoid a grilling.

"Ol' Gus cut his hand this morning. Had to bring him in for stitches."

Michael narrowed his eyes. Ol' Gus had hands like shoe leather. "I thought you did all the doctoring at your place."

"Gus needed a tetanus shot." Elijah grinned. "Now, you're not gettin' all suspicious that I was following you to the scene of the crime, are you?"

Michael wouldn't put it past him. "Guess without Gus you're shorthanded. Better get on home, then."

Elijah's grin widened and his drawl thickened. "And miss this opportunity to give my congratulations in person? You coulda told a fella, you know. No need to leave a lyin' message that you were stayin' in last night."

Michael sighed. "It was a chance encounter, okay?"

"You mean like fate?"

Michael sighed again. "I mean like an act of human kindness. Lay off, will you? My grandfather already had at me this morning."

Elijah laughed and waved the newspaper. "Joseph got wind of this already?"

"Would you doubt it? God, I wish he'd just come back to Oklahoma and put his nose into Wentworth Oil Works and keep it out of my business."

Elijah snorted. "The only way you're going to get that old man back at his desk is if you leave yours. C'mon. That parcel of land you bought next to mine is ready and waiting. Let's go into partnership and build the best quarter horse stable in the country."

Michael ran his hands through his hair. "For the damnzillionth time, Elijah, I don't have the cash. Thanks to Grandfather, who made me agree to take my Wentworth Oil Works salary in stock and to that neat and tidy little trust fund that has my money until I'm thirty or married."

Elijah shook his head. "Maybe marriage isn't such a bad idea, friend." He brought the newspaper up, photo-to-nose with Michael. "Look at the kind of trouble you're getting into as a single guy."

The picture wasn't a half-bad shot of Beth. While the black-and-white did nothing for her pale coloring, her delicate features were clearly shown. The baby still looked like a peanut with limbs to him, though.

The baby.

"You want to hear what she named him?" he asked Elijah, again anticipating a rise of anger and irritation. "She named him after me. She named the baby Michael." He crossed his arms over his chest. "What do you think about that?"

Elijah blinked, blinked again, and then continued staring at Michael, astonishment, puzzlement, and then amusement working across his face. "You want to know what I really think?" Elijah laughed, shaking his head. "I think you better make an honest woman of her. Hey, then you can dump the pinstripes and you and I can really rock the Rockin' H."

What the hell was up with Elijah? Marry Beth? And why was he laughing when Michael was irritated, possibly even incensed, about the whole baby business?

It took just another moment to figure it out. The moment when he caught sight of his reflection in the chrome top of the nearest newsstand. Though his rational, bachelor mind said he should be irritated, or angry, or yes, even incensed, his face had split into a loony grin—as if he were actually, truly, indeed, the proudest of papas.

Beth placed her almost three-week-old son gently back in his crib after his 5:30 a.m. feeding just as a gentle knock on her front door sounded. It would be Bea Hansen, who invariably came from the bakery to the studio apartment upstairs with a hot cup of coffee and warm baked goods. The bakery business made early risers.

The gray-haired woman crossed the threshold with a cardboard tray holding two steaming paper cups and two delicious-smelling muffins.

Beth sniffed with appreciation. "You spoil me." She smiled and gestured to the worn love seat in one corner of the apartment. "Come sit."

Bea scrutinized Beth's face as they sat down on the floral cushions. "You don't look as peaked this morning. The 2:00 a.m. feeding go well?"

"Fine." Beth held the coffee beneath her nose and inhaled the aroma. "Now that I've found the overnight news service on TV." She nodded in the direction of her little black-and-white on the kitchenette countertop.

Bea smiled, laughter lines bracketing the caring in her eyes. "I remember how lonely those night feedings can be."

"Hm." Beth sipped the coffee. *Lonely.*

Bea's smile dissolved. "You're worrying me again, dear. No husband, no mother—"

"I have the baby." *Lonely.* He had to be enough, because she would never have a mother. As for a husband...

"But without family to—"

Beth interrupted Bea again by touching the older woman's hand. "One loyal friend is worth ten thousand relatives.''

Bea squared her shoulders. ''Then you have twenty thousand in Millie and me, but you won't let us help you.''

Beth had to smile at that. ''What do you mean? You gave me a job and a place to live.''

''We're paying you just over minimum wage for counter help and bookwork.''

''You're giving me much-needed experience.'' Beth took another sip from her cup. ''And don't forget breakfast.''

''But we're kicking you out of your apartment.''

Beth waved away the concern. ''This was going to be Millie's mother's place. You two told me that from the beginning, Bea.''

The older woman humphed. ''If only—'' Bea broke off and shook her head, a familiar, speculative light gleaming in her eyes. She swung around to look at the *Daily Post* photo that Beth had framed and hung on the wall between the crib and her own single bed. ''Yes. If only Michael Wentworth—''

Beth's heart bumped into her throat. ''Don't start now,'' she warned the older woman. Bea and Millie, sweet gossips that they were, invented stories where there were none. And for some reason they'd latched on to an imaginary romance between Beth and Michael. ''That poor man was just doing me a favor.''

While the photo and accompanying article had garnered her and the baby boxes of donated diapers, baby clothes and baby food, Beth realized that the only thing Michael had received from the publicity was embarrassment. Bea and Millie's bakery attracted a huge segment of the Freemont Springs population, and their customers had brought her good wishes as well as the news that Michael Wentworth was desperate to recover his bachelor reputation.

And from the bakery regulars she'd also learned that despite her tip, the Wentworth family still hadn't found Sabrina.

"Well," Bea said, getting up from the love seat and crossing over to look at the photo, "I still say Michael Wentworth could use some settling down."

"*Bea,* you know I'm not interested in him—" Beth quickly shut her mouth as she spied an incriminating piece of evidence peeking out from beneath the pillows of her unmade bed.

Michael Wentworth's sheepskin jacket.

She stood, too, but didn't make any quick movements toward the bed. Bea would be sure to spy the jacket then, and Beth had told her days ago that she'd returned it.

She'd meant to, especially after Bea had found her one day wrapped in the soft suede and sheepskin while nursing the baby. Beth had come across it on her first night home from the hospital and had thrown it around her shoulders during the 2:00 a.m. feeding. Through the thin flannel of her nightgown she'd found the soft warmth of the sheep's wool liner comforting.

Beth edged closer to her bed. If Bea knew she still had the jacket, her matchmaking efforts might possibly start in earnest. As for more matchmaking *conversation*—definitely.

She eyed the jacket again. Would it be better to try to stuff the darn thing completely beneath the pillows or nudge it gently to the floor on the far side of the bed?

"Tell me again about this new place to live you found." Bea turned away from the photo on the wall. "One half of a duplex, you said?"

Beth stilled and willed herself not to look at the telltale jacket. "I'm lucky to get it." She was. Inexpensive apartments in prosperous Freemont Springs were limited. "Mr. Stanley seems nice."

"Once you promised you wouldn't make noise, overuse the lights or heat and have no more than one bag of garbage each week."

Beth sighed. There *was* that little concern. The crotchety man had quite a few rules that she and the baby had better not break. Goodness, she hoped disposable diapers could be crushed like aluminum cans.

Bea's sigh echoed hers. "You need a man, and I don't mean Ralph Stanley."

Need a man? No way would Beth risk her heart again, not after how Evan had left at the first sign of responsibility. "I have the only man I need, and he's three weeks old and sleeping like an angel." She couldn't help her smile.

Bea smiled back. "Your boy *is* an angel." She scooted to stand beside the crib.

Beth edged closer to the head of her bed. The sleeve of Michael Wentworth's jacket emerged from beneath two plumped-up pillows. Her fingers closed over the soft suede.

"What have we here?"

Bea's voice made Beth jump. She whirled toward the woman, blocking the sight of the jacket with her body. In Bea's fingers was a pacifier.

Beth swallowed. "Oh, that was part of the New Year's Baby bounty." She shook her head. "The baby doesn't like it."

"My *husband* didn't like our children sucking on pacifiers."

Beth sank down onto the mattress while at the same time quickly pushing up the blankets to cover the jacket. She smiled. "At least I don't have that worry." Beneath the sheets, her hands slid against the soft inside fleece. By habit, she found herself twining her fingers through it.

Bea gazed at Beth, shaking her head. "You're braver than I ever was."

Beth pretended not to understand. "A widow who went on to create a successful business? Bea, you're the one with courage!"

Gray curls wiggled back and forth. "But I had my husband to help me raise the children. A man to love me and to love the babies."

Beth gripped the wool tighter. "I'm fine, Bea." *Never admit to anything but that.*

Another sigh escaped the older woman. "I have to get back to the shop," she said reluctantly.

With relief, Beth watched Bea adjust the sleeping baby's blanket and then cross the room toward the door. "Goodbye, Bea," Beth said. "I'll be in for my shift this afternoon."

At the door, Bea paused with her hand on the

knob. "Aren't you lonely, dear?" she asked quietly. "It's no sin to admit to that."

But it is.

After years of practice Beth's smile brightened automatically. "Fine, Bea. I'm just fine."

The door clicked shut behind the older woman.

Involuntarily, Beth pulled the jacket from beneath the pillows and buried her face in the soft, comforting folds. It smelled like Michael Wentworth, a male fragrance that worked like a magic charm to dispel—

She refused to think the word.

"Loneliness." It whispered out of her mouth instead.

Loneliness...loneliness...loneliness. The dreaded thought echoed against the four walls until Beth wanted to slap her hands over her ears.

She pushed the jacket off her lap and left it lying on the floor instead. Maybe the jacket was to blame for her uncharacteristic weakness. There had been doubts in the middle of the night. An emptiness she sensed inside, even when she held her much-loved child in her arms.

The jacket had to go. Today.

Because Beth Masterson never admitted to loneliness.

3

With a leery eye on the new stack of files on his desk, Michael sat down in his executive chair at Wentworth Oil Works. With one thumb and forefinger, he flicked the first couple of manila folders, causing the stack to topple and spread over the entire mahogany surface.

He breathed a sigh of relief. Nothing hidden there. No rattles, no bubble gum cigars, no pamphlets on baby burping or baby barfing.

Nothing baby at all.

Another exhale whooshed out. It might have taken three weeks, but it had finally happened.

No more daddy jokes.

He gathered up the papers, restacking them, then immediately wished he hadn't. Hell, where did all this stuff come from? One meeting away from the office and the paperwork and the hassles and the headaches multiplied like fleas on a dog.

Damn Grandfather.

The old man had taken off to Washington again, leaving Wentworth Oil Works in what Joseph termed Michael's "capable" hands. Capable, hell. Maybe he should appreciate the confidence, but not when

Grandfather refused to see how *reluctant* those hands were.

The old man was blind when he wanted to be and a master manipulator all of the time. A headache started behind Michael's eyes. Unless he could find a way to force Joseph back to his desk, he had a feeling he might be chained to this one for the rest of his life.

He glanced at the memo on top of the stack. "To Mr. Michael Wentworth, Wentworth Oil Works." *Wentworth.* Dammit, every day the name, the responsibilities, his entire family, for Pete's sake, weighed him down like a curse.

Bzzz.

Michael pressed the intercom button. "Thank you, Lisa," he said to his assistant through the speaker, "for interrupting one of the more depressing moments of my life."

Lisa didn't snap back with her usual sassiness. "Uh, sir—"

She *never* called him sir. "What is it?"

A pregnant pause. "Visitors for you, sir, uh, two."

Lisa's "pregnant" pause was explained when she ushered in his unscheduled visitors. Two people he wanted to see in his office only slightly less than the IRS.

He groaned. Out loud. Because now that the daddy jokes were dying down at last, he just *knew* they'd be starting right back up again.

Visitor number one: Ensconced but asleep in a dilapidated but clean-looking stroller, a snow-suited Michael Freemont Masterson. Visitor number two:

Beth, in her ragged blue parka, a red woolen scarf wrapping her head and throat, Michael's own sheepskin coat tucked under one arm.

She smiled tentatively. "I brought your coat back. I'm sorry it's taken me so long."

He glanced at his watch. What if the visit lasted a mere forty-five seconds? Heck, maybe nobody would even hear of it then. He sent a glare in the direction of Lisa, who hovered in the doorway. *Don't spill a word of this,* he silently commanded her, and reached out to take the coat. *Now show the nice lady out.*

Apparently completely missing his signals, Lisa darted forward and snatched the jacket. "Sit down, sit down, Ms. Masterson. Can I get you something? Tea? Coffee?"

Michael's jaw dropped. Lisa didn't bring anybody anything. If *he* wanted coffee, he schlepped to the outer office and poured his own cup.

Beth smiled at Lisa as though she understood the honor conferred upon her. "A cup of tea? Please. Just a little to warm my hands."

"You should wear gloves," Michael heard himself say, frowning at her bare fingers. Then, in a voice still surly, he found himself adding, "I guess you can sit down."

He frowned again as she wheeled the stroller alongside the visitor's chair across from his desk. How long could "just a little" tea take? Ninety seconds, tops.

With quick movements she unzipped her jacket and pulled the scarf off her head. The parka dropped to the chair.

Michael stared, not quite knowing what part of her made it so hard for him to look away. She'd been wearing coats or gowns or blankets when he'd seen her before. She'd been wearing a long fall of pale blond hair, too.

"You cut it," he said stupidly.

"Easier this way." She ran her hand over her close-cropped hair. Though slightly longer than a boy's, the short style hugged the contours of her head. It swept softly around her face, making her eyes appear incredibly big and her mouth temptingly full.

"Sit down, sit down." Not wanting to notice anything more about her face, or what she looked like below it, he waved her into the seat just as Lisa came back with a steaming cup.

His assistant took a moment to admire the baby before turning her attention to Beth. She handed over the tea. "You couldn't have had a baby three weeks ago," Lisa said with a smile. "Nobody gets her figure back that quickly."

Okay, so he looked then. He'd tried not to, but it was Lisa's fault. Yeah, before Beth had worn parkas and gowns and blankets. Now it was faded blue jeans and a tight-fitting off-white ski sweater.

Beth smiled again at Lisa. "I've always been on the skinny side. Believe me, some of these curves are brand-new."

Now it was Beth's fault he was looking. Yes, there was a natural slenderness about her. But if those curves were a recent acquisition, then childbirth was this lady's best friend.

He suddenly realized that both women were looking at him. God, had he made some sound? Hell, had he *moaned?*

Clearing his throat, he made a point of looking at his watch again. He couldn't remember when Beth had arrived, but obviously she'd been here too long.

She took a sip of tea and the hint. "I should be going. I have to get back to the bakery."

"The bakery?" Michael frowned and watched Lisa slip from the room and shut his office door. "That's right. You said you worked there. You're not back on the job already?"

She rose to her feet. "Bea and Millie need me."

An unfamiliar discomfort edged down his spine. "You need rest. Bea and Millie can do without you a while longer."

Her smile was polite as she carefully set the cup on the edge of his desk. "Thank you again for the loan of the jacket—and everything else you did for me."

He didn't like her heading out into the cold just yet. "Don't you want to know about Sabrina?"

She paused in picking up her ratty parka.

"Is that jacket warm enough? Would you like to keep the sheepskin one?"

She shook her head vehemently. "What about Sabrina?"

"Thanks to you, we found out she *was* in town. Even where she was staying." Guilt ran through him. He should have stopped by and told Beth what they'd discovered. Brought something for the kid. But he'd been so determined to quash the rumors flying around town that he'd avoided anything to do with her. "Sabrina's disappeared again, though."

In the process of zipping her coat, Beth's hands stilled. "Oh, I'm sorry. I hope you find her." She dug into her pocket and fished out some keys.

Michael thought of Beth driving back to the bakery. "Is your car heater still on the fritz? I could have someone—"

"It's working again." She wound the scarf around her neck.

"You don't have time for a longer visit?" He didn't know what the hell prompted him to say that.

She cocked her head and looked at his cluttered desk. "Looks to me like *you* don't have time for a longer visit."

He followed her gaze. "That. It's nothing." Just the leash that chained him to the Oil Works. "You haven't even told me about your son." Michael looked at the still-sleeping baby. His face was rounder now, and as Michael watched the baby's lips pursed and made sucking motions.

"I call him Mischa."

Strange, the disappointment that stabbed him. "You changed his name," Michael said.

Beth shook her head. "No, it's just a nickname. The Slavic form of yours."

She wheeled the shabby stroller toward the door, and he noticed that one wheel listed to the side. He couldn't think of another reason for her to stay.

"You didn't want to call him Michael?" The stupid question just popped out.

Her back to him, she paused. Then she looked over

her shoulder and he saw color in her cheeks that matched the heart red scarf around her neck. "I guess I thought that there was only one of those," she said before leaving.

From his office windows, Michael watched Beth transfer the baby from the stroller to her car and drive away. Then he slowly walked through his door to the outer office. Lisa stood by the fax machine.

His secretary was married and had a couple of kids. He remembered her taking maternity leave each time. Something like three months. Maybe more.

"Isn't a woman supposed to take it easy after she has a baby?"

Lisa picked up the fax and quickly scanned it. "After giving birth, a woman deserves a maid and her mother for at least six months."

"She's not supposed to start work right away then."

Lisa shrugged. "Maybe she doesn't have any choice. A woman might need the money."

Ratty coat. Stroller with listing wheels. Car with unreliable heater. "I don't like it," Michael muttered.

"Oh, boss, you're going to not like this even more." Lisa smacked the fax against his hand.

Michael took it, still thinking of Beth and Mischa. He read it once, started, read through it again.

Joseph Wentworth was proposing naming Michael Wentworth Acting CEO of Wentworth Oil Works. Jack's old job.

Damn.

Michael crumpled the fax in his fist. The old bastard. He thought he'd permanently tie Michael to the company and the family so easily.

"He's not going to get away with it, Lisa."

She looked skeptical. "Don't know what you're going to do about it, boss."

Michael three-pointed the balled paper into the trash can beside Lisa's desk. His gaze snagged on her In box. Another photocopy of that three-week-old *Daily Post* photo. Somebody had drawn a cartoon bubble over his head in the picture. He didn't bother reading what was written inside.

Great. A three-minute visit and the jokes were starting up again already.

That was the last thing he needed. Acting CEO and more speculation about the end of his bachelorhood.

The end of his bachelorhood. Michael froze, an Einstein-caliber idea crystalizing in his mind. Okay, Elijah had mentioned it first, but Michael was the only one who could make it a reality.

"Wentworth, you *are* a genius," he whispered to himself. "With this idea everybody wins."

Half an hour to carefully consider the idea. Ten minutes to the Freemont Springs Bakery. One and a half minutes to find out that Beth was in her apartment and to knock on the door at the top of the stairs.

Only an instant more and she opened the door.

With the January cold at his back and her puzzled expression facing him, Michael cut right to the chase. "Marry me," he said.

Beth stared at Michael, not even taking in his words, only aware of the threadbare robe wrapped around her shower-wet body and the dual drops of chilly water escaping from the towel turban to roll down her neck.

Did the man take some kind of sadistic pleasure in barging in on her when she wasn't at her best? At least she'd been in her favorite jeans and sweater when she'd visited his office, but upon her arrival home, Mischa had spit up all over her neck and shoulder—requiring the day's second shower.

Come to think of it, she should be surprised Michael had caught her *after* the spit up.

"Did you hear what I said?" He stepped over the threshold and closed the door behind him, bringing him closer than she liked.

She stepped back, her hands tightening the sash at her waist. In a dark suit and muted tie he looked like the board members who had visited the orphanage from time to time, not a man who'd just proposed marriage.

Marriage? Beth swallowed and took another step back. "What did you say?"

"I asked you to marry me."

Beneath her pink-striped robe, chills trailed down her arms from shoulders to wrists. "You didn't ask," she stated, replaying the words in her head. "I think you just said, 'Marry me.'"

"Right." He grinned.

The smile tossed her insides like confetti. Beth crossed her arms over her chest, hugging herself to warm away a second swathe of goose bumps. "This isn't making sense," she said. She glanced toward the crib where Mischa made the little grunting noises that signaled he was waking up.

"Makes perfect sense," Michael answered. Without asking, he strode across the room and dropped onto the flowery love seat, his long legs and wide shoulders taking over the only seating in the room. "Everybody wins."

Beth crossed to the crib and took Mischa in her arms before his grunts became a full-blown cry. He blinked at her and she rubbed her nose against his. "Hi, baby," she whispered to give herself another minute.

Holding Mischa against her heart like armor, she faced Michael. "I'm not following. What exactly are you talking about?"

He slapped his hands against his thighs and jumped up from the love seat. "It's because I'm just so damn happy with the idea." He grinned again. "I should have thought of this weeks ago."

Damn happy? He appeared that way, boyish and delighted, and a little thrill rushed through her. How long had it been since a man looked at her like that? Laughing, excited, as if she were the one he wanted. She ran the conversation through her mind again.

He wanted to *marry* her, he said.

She put Mischa in the infant seat on the tiny coffee table then self-consciously tugged the towel from her hair. "I'm sorry...I just got out of the shower."

He wanted to marry *her,* he said.

That boyish grin widened on his face. "I don't care what you look like. I just want to get your name on a marriage certificate."

Marriage. Belonging to someone. Making a family with Michael and Mischa. Dreams she'd thought long dried up bloomed instantly in her mind. "You can't mean it," she whispered, though her imagination put him in her home, her bed, his strong hands touching the pale skin of her body. Even though Michael was a near-stranger, the image made her stomach quiver.

"Of course I mean it. You. Me. Marriage of convenience. Isn't that what they call it?"

Lord, his good humor was so infectious she almost smiled back. Then reality set in. "A *marriage of convenience?*"

"Right. We'll sign an ironclad prenup, but then we'll marry, I'll get out of the company, get the trust, get the ranch, and finally give you your freedom and enough cash that you and Mischa will be set for life."

Again, he said it all with such certainty that she nearly agreed. "Wait a minute." She rubbed the towel briskly through her wet hair as if that might rub some sense back into the conversation. "And you also have some oceanfront Oklahoma property to sell me, I presume?"

With one stride he was before her. "I've got a cantankerous, patriarchal grandfather who refuses to see he belongs at the head of the family business and I don't, okay?" Michael speared his fingers through his hair. "I've got to force his hand or else he'll make himself sick looking into my brother Jack's death and he'll make me nuts tying me to a desk at Wentworth Oil."

Beth had heard about Jack Wentworth's untimely death. She'd even been aware of Joseph Wentworth's reputation as a stubborn but successful businessman. "I still don't get how I fit in." Why had Michael come to her?

"Just more of the Wentworth ties that bind—a trust fund I can't get to for three more years. Unless I'm married."

Then he told her about the ranching operation he wanted to go into with his friend Elijah. Quarter horses. Studs. What she knew about ranching came from late-night TV Westerns, yet the unleashed enthusiasm in his voice painted a vivid picture of his dream.

"And where am I in all this again?" she asked, finally surfacing from his deluge.

He held his hands out at his sides, smiling once more. "The temporary wife."

Beth swallowed. "You don't think a marriage should be for—" she twisted the towel in her fists "—love?"

Grimacing, Michael waved the thought away. "Save the sap for greeting cards."

"You don't—"

"Don't say any more," he said. "Just think. My grandfather gets what he needs. I get what I need. You get what you need."

And what exactly is that? Beth thought. She wrung the towel again. "I don't see—"

"That's the problem." Michael grabbed the loose end of the towel in her hands and tugged her closer to him. "You're not seeing what I'm seeing."

His eyes were a deep brown ringed in gold. He smelled like the sheepskin jacket had—warm, exciting, *male*. "And how is that?" Beth asked, licking her lips to wet them. "How is it that you see me?" She *felt* suddenly womanly and feminine and as if the world were lying on its side. Air couldn't find her lungs.

Suddenly, he dropped his end of the towel and backed away. "As a person who could use some help." Another step back and his gaze searched the room to light on Mischa. "As a mother with a baby—my namesake—to take care of."

The world righted itself after that. The whole thing became clear. Michael wanted a convenient, *temporary* wife and he'd thought of her. Because of Mischa. Because he pitied her. He hadn't seen her as an individual, as a *woman* at all.

Well, she'd taken handouts for the first eighteen years of her life. Five years ago she'd sworn never to do it again.

She was relieved to discover that Michael took no for an answer quite politely.

Michael halted at the bottom of the stairs to Beth's apartment.

What the hell is wrong with me?

He never took no for an answer.

Maybe it was her short hairstyle that put him off his game. Or the distracting scent of soap on her naked skin. That thin robe—

He groaned and shoved his hands into his trouser pockets. To be this close and then to lose it!

Where had he gone wrong? Hadn't he laid out the advantages? Explained that it would be a temporary commitment ending in financial security for her and Mischa?

Ask her again. His business-school-honed senses urged him back up the stairs.

And some other instinct warned him away.

A beautiful woman. A child carrying his name. Hell, even if they stayed married just a few months, how difficult would it be to regain his bachelor status?

Easy, his common sense responded. Wentworths never had trouble with women.

And that other talking instinct snickered. *There's always a first time.*

Still undecided, Michael heard the telephone ring in Beth's apartment upstairs, followed by Mischa's cry. Michael found himself halfway up the steps by the time the phone stopped ringing and Beth was calling "Hello?" over the increasing wail of the baby.

Outside the flimsy apartment door he heard her end of the conversation with a Mr. Stanley, obviously a would-be landlord. Even with only one half of the conversation audible, Michael could tell Mr. Stanley wasn't a patient man.

He didn't want to let her call him back later.

He wanted to know if the baby cried like that often.

There was also something about diapers and garbage that made absolutely no sense.

And finally he heard Beth lose out on what apparently had been the only Freemont Springs apartment available in her price range.

A more polite man wouldn't have eavesdropped.

A kinder man would have let her face her trouble privately.

But Michael hadn't grown up at Joseph Wentworth's manipulative knee for nothing.

He knocked again on Beth's door and went for the throat.

Her face looked paler than it had a few minutes ago. She stared at him, dazed. "I wanted Mischa to grow up here," she said as he walked in and shut the door. "Freemont is his middle name because I wanted him never to forget where he belongs."

Michael touched her elbow to guide her to the tiny couch. She sat down without any other prompting, the baby curled in the curve of her arm.

"You like it here, then?" he said casually.

"My car blew two tires just outside of town. It had made it all the way from L.A., asking only for gas, oil and water until I passed the sign saying Entering Freemont Springs." One hand fluttered. "Then *poof!*" She grimaced. "Or should I say *pop?*"

"You decided to stay?"

She nodded. "I didn't have the money for a pair of tires. And Alice always said that when you break an egg you better make an omelette."

Michael let Alice and the omelette thing go. "And Mischa's the New Year's baby. Freemont Springs is his town."

She frowned. "I thought so. It's so family-friendly

here. It felt so right for us. But I just lost the only place I've found to live that I can afford.''

He hated her unhappiness. ''There's always that simple solution.''

Her eyebrows were silky blond and came together in a frown. ''What simple solution?''

''Marry me, Beth,'' he said quietly.

''That's simple?''

Even though her eyelashes hid her gaze, he thought she softened. He didn't know how he knew, but something flowed between them, something that had started that night when he held her hands in the hospital. Maybe it began before that, when her finger had touched his cheek. Or when he'd first seen her moonlight hair.

''Just temporarily.'' He swallowed at the hoarseness in his voice. ''But you'll end up with enough money so you can stay. Do it for Mischa, Beth.'' He went in for the kill. ''So Mischa can belong to his town.''

She looked up. The turquoise blue of her eyes startled him again. ''I don't know.'' The baby had drifted off against her shoulder and she walked over to the crib, the most luxurious item in the room. Mischa snuggled down without a whimper.

Beth slowly turned to face Michael. The apartment was so small she seemed only an arm's length away. She pursed her lips. ''Alice did always say that when opportunity's at the door to open it widely....''

Michael rapped an imaginary door. ''Knock knock.''

She looked back at the baby. She looked at him.

Say yes, Michael willed.

"Yes."

In a strange flood of relief and anticipation, that arm's length between them disappeared. His hands wrapped around Beth's upper arms—too thin, he registered. He brought her against his chest, her breasts full against him, and his mouth touched the corner of her lips.

That's all.

That wasn't enough. Because she inhaled a surprised breath, and somehow the sound was excited, exciting, and his mouth moved and her lips softened and he was truly kissing her.

$$4$$

Marry in haste, repent at leisure. Alice, the woman who had taken care of the children in Beth's age group at the Thurston Home for Girls, had never spoken that particular adage, but it echoed in Beth's head nonetheless. Maybe because now, five days after Michael's proposal and two hours after their 3:00 p.m. city hall wedding, she finally had time to listen to herself think.

Her thoughts weren't joyful.

In the Wentworth mansion—more like castle—bedroom designated for the baby, Beth dug into the paper shopping bag for more of Mischa's tiny clothes. The Wentworth housekeeper, Evelyn, hadn't raised an eyebrow at Beth's "luggage," a worn duffel bag and two shopping bags, nor her expressed wish to put the baby's clothes away herself. Not only was she unaccustomed to being waited upon, but she needed to close herself in a corner of this monstrous home to quiet her heartbeat and get her bearings.

Had she made a mistake as cavernously sized as this house?

She peeked over at Mischa, sleeping soundly in his familiar crib. She'd brought that with her—her one extravagance—and its fancy turned spindles didn't look out of place in the peach-walled room with a deep window seat and an oriental carpet covering most of the gleaming wood floor.

But did she and Mischa belong here?

The room held the faint scent of the cedar lining the closet where she'd hung her own meager wardrobe. And the marble-topped, ornately carved dresser had plenty of space for both Mischa's clothes and her underthings. The brass daybed in the room would be a fine place for her to sleep.

The bed made her think of Michael. She gritted her teeth and slapped a stack of tiny undershirts in the bottom of the drawer. She'd accepted a "convenient"—temporary and sexless—marriage. That first wild thought when he'd proposed, that he'd be in her life and bed forever—had died quickly, like every other of her romantic notions.

She should be used to disappointment by now.

A year ago she'd led with her needy heart. Unwary, she'd fallen for the first warm smile and outstretched hand. But her solo pregnancy had callused every urge that wasn't maternal.

So she needn't worry. She'd gone into this arrangement with Michael eyes open. For the sake of her son's future and security. Beth determinedly placed the last of Mischa's clothes in the dresser. Then, with the paper bag luggage in her hands, all ready to be crushed then tossed in the garbage, she froze.

"I'll need them again," she said aloud softly. It was true. "Soon." Folded crisply and carefully, the bags were stashed neatly beside her duffel in the good-smelling closet. A small sigh of relief escaped as she regarded the easily accessible getaway bags.

How would she handle the strangeness of this situation, this marriage? How could she protect the new calluses? Never again would she be caught unwary or unprepared.

Mischa was awake and being diaper changed when a brisk tap sounded at the door. Beth's heart started a bad-engine knock-and-wheeze in her chest. That wasn't Evelyn's knock. That was Michael's knock.

Her husband's knock.

She tried clearing her tight throat. "Come in."

Michael opened the door and stepped inside. He'd dropped her off at the house after the brief wedding—not witnessed by any of the Wentworths, but rather two friends, because he said he wanted to surprise his family after the fact—and headed back to his office. He still wore the same dark suit and muted tie. The ring she'd surprised him with glittered on his left hand.

He was absently rolling the band around his finger with his thumb. She'd avoided mooning over her own ring, a wide circle of gold embellished with rows of seed pearls and polished teardrops of turquoise. Michael had mumbled a surprising something about his choice being inspired by her golden hair and glowing eyes.

He spoke into the heavy silence. "You're doing okay?" No smile softened his mouth.

Beth's heart banged against her chest harder than ever. "Fine. Both Mischa and I are fine." Since picking her up for the wedding, Michael's elated and satisfied mood of the days before had dissolved. It appeared as if maybe for good.

But a smile overtook his face as he looked at Mischa. "How is the little guy this evening?" Michael walked a few steps toward the brass bed where the baby lay swaddled in a blanket.

Beth smiled herself. "He doesn't seem a bit intimidated by his new quarters in the magnificent and endless Wentworth mansion."

Michael's finger stroked Mischa's cheek, but his eyes turned on her. "And you? Are you intimidated?"

By the house, no. By the man standing beside me, yes. She shrugged.

He turned back to Mischa and let the baby catch his finger for a squeeze. Michael smiled again. "And you, are you unpacked?" he asked casually. "Evelyn said you wanted to do it yourself."

His shoulder brushed hers as he made a play at arm-and-finger wrestling with Mischa. Suddenly, Beth realized Michael was too close. Even though they'd agreed their marriage was to be temporary and sexless, right now, with the door closed, his body brushing hers, his presence felt too intimate.

"About, uh, about my room…" Right away she'd make clear that she planned to sleep here. Evelyn had shown her to Michael's room, just across the hall, and she'd smiled but turned hurriedly away from the masculine furnishings and his all-male, all-seductive football field of a bed. Did their "convenient'' marriage mean he expected her to share that with him—temporarily? Sexlessly?

Just make clear you won't.

"What are these?" Michael's voice startled her. He'd moved away from the daybed to stand at the small writing desk. A stack of *Business Week* magazines topped by today's *Wall Street Journal* lay centered on the desk's leather-bound blotter.

Glad to be momentarily distracted from the discussion of sleeping arrangements, Beth sat beside Mischa on the bed and gently stroked his hair. "Reading material I should catch up on."

Michael's ringed, left hand flipped quickly through the densely packed text of one of the magazines. "You subscribe to these?" He frowned. "I guess I don't know much about you."

Now would be a fine time to tell him all he needed to know was that she wouldn't sleep with him. Period. Even with a promise of no sex.

"I was attending one of the state universities in L.A.," she said instead. Until Evan, Mischa's father and one of the grad students in the business department, had denied all responsibility for the baby. Apparently he was such a believer in statistics that he couldn't accept they'd been caught by the small failure rate of their birth control method.

"I'm three semesters away from a degree. Accounting major." Though maybe she should have majored in fairy tales, Beth thought. Because despite her lonely childhood—or maybe because of it— she'd believed in them right up to the minute when

Evan said he hadn't really loved her after all and then accused her of trying to trap him. *Yeah, some prince.*

But bitterness wasn't a healthy emotion for a single mother. Squaring her shoulders, she blocked off thoughts of Evan and his eight-month-old defection and looked Michael deliberately, calmly, straight in the eye.

Well, her stomach danced as if it heard a hip-hop beat, but she didn't think he could see that. "About sleeping together—"

Groan. Did she really say that? Well, if Michael's startled face was any judge, she had. "I mean, about the sleeping *arrangements.*"

His full attention focused on her now. The gold rings edging the irises of his dark eyes reminded her of the band she'd placed on his finger this afternoon. His skin had been cool, his fingers steady, but he'd squeezed her hand tightly after they'd exchanged rings.

She stared at his mouth. He'd kissed her, too. Nothing like that heated caress that had come after she'd agreed to marry him. The mere memory started a hot shiver running down her spine. But that passion had just been a symptom of his exuberance at outfoxing his grandfather. Their kiss in the city hall had been brief, cool, in control.

She'd hated it.

"The sleeping arrangements?" Michael prompted. He slid his hands in his trouser pockets and leaned against the desk, crossing one foot over the other. Cool and in control.

But then she saw the faint tick in his jaw, as if he

were struggling for the casual pose and attitude. His gaze, almost hot now, licked over her face. Another shiver melted Beth's spine.

Tell him you won't be sleeping with him.

"I'll be staying in here," she burst out, one hand moving to grip a rail of the brass bed. "In here with Mischa." She squeezed the cool metal in her fist, as if she needed to hold on…or maybe hold out.

That tick in Michael's jaw pounded. He straightened away from the desk and moved toward her. Beth gripped the daybed tighter.

His hot eyes ran over her, from her face to her chest, then down her jeans and back up to her face. Beth's breath disappeared.

"That's best," he said, his voice mild in comparison to the warmth in his gaze and the hard tautness of his shoulders.

He crossed quickly to the door. "Fine with me." It shut behind him.

Beth unlocked her fingers from the daybed's brass rail. She massaged her stiff hand and stared at the beautiful ring wrapped around her finger.

And tried to figure out why his casual acceptance of her proclamation—which should have been a tremendous relief—seemed like just one more disappointment.

If the Wentworth mansion was a castle, Beth decided as she descended the massive staircase the next morning, then she was the princess who'd suffered the night with a pea beneath her mattress.

She hadn't slept for an instant in the daybed.

Instead, she'd listened to Mischa's baby rustles and baby breaths and counted the stars on the backsides of her eyelids. She yawned and dragged the fatigue after her down the hallway. At breakfast, she'd avoid coffee and then head right back upstairs with Mischa for a morning nap.

The sight of Michael, clear-eyed and with shower-damp hair, seated at the breakfast room table made her swallow her next yawn.

"Good morning," he said over the newspaper he held.

"Morning," Beth replied. She'd hoped to avoid him altogether by dashing in for an early breakfast. Before she could think up an excuse and head back to her room, Evelyn pushed through a swinging door with a steaming basket.

"Let me take the baby while you eat, Mrs. Wentworth." In one movement, the housekeeper set down the basket, pulled out the chair opposite Michael's and scooped up Mischa in her arms.

Mrs. Wentworth? Startled, Beth blinked and sat down as Evelyn swept back to the kitchen.

"Coffee, Mrs. Wentworth?"

Beth jumped. An older woman in a plain dress and apron materialized from a corner with a shining silver coffeepot. Apparently taking silence as agreement, the woman filled a dainty china cup and then also retreated through the swinging door.

Beth blinked again. *Mrs. Wentworth?* She looked down at her ringed finger. Of course, Mrs. Wentworth.

The newspaper rattled. "Thought it was all a

dream, huh?'' Over the edge of the newspaper, Michael's expression gave away nothing. ''But then you woke up to find you are indeed my wife.''

Beth shut her mouth with an audible snap. *His wife. Servants. Mrs. Wentworth.* Nothing at the Thurston Home for Girls had prepared her for this new role. ''Temporary wife,'' she said, and a temporary role she'd handle by hiding away as much as possible—from the servants *and* Michael. From the whole world.

After breakfast she'd retreat to her room for that nap. From now on she'd scrounge her meals in the kitchen at odd hours. ''Temporary wife,'' she said again firmly.

He slid a glance toward the kitchen. ''Don't let that get around.'' He folded the newspaper and set it beside his plate. ''Especially since I spoke with my grandfather last night.''

Ways of keeping the lowest of profiles still occupied Beth's brain. ''I thought you already told him,'' she said absently.

Michael smiled grimly. ''I couldn't reach him before—only his voice mail. But we spoke person-to-person last night.''

Something in his voice snagged Beth's full attention. ''And?'' Her agreement with Michael hinged upon his grandfather, Joseph Wentworth, buying into their marriage. Suddenly, she didn't know what she hoped for most—that he did or he didn't. ''And he took the news—?''

Michael shrugged. ''Well. I might say suspiciously

well, if I didn't know how distracted he is by finding out exactly what happened to Jack.''

At his brother's name, tension crossed Michael's face. Beth couldn't miss the sudden tightening of his mouth. With deliberate casualness, she reached for her coffee cup and stared into the fragrant blackness. A real wife might try to comfort him. A convenient wife kept her mouth shut. ''What about your resignation? Did you also tell him you were leaving the Oil Works?''

Michael shot her a strange look. ''Are you looking out for me?''

''For myself,'' she corrected quickly. ''That's our bargain, remember? You get out of the family business and I get security for Mischa.''

Michael shrugged again. ''He took that fine, too. I've been telling him for months that Steve Donnolly can do the job, and for the first time he agreed with me.''

''So it's done then.'' Beth brought the coffee to her lips. Now all she had to do was take Mischa upstairs to wait out this sham of a marriage.

''Maybe.''

She set cup to saucer with a clatter. ''What do you mean, maybe?''

Michael made another precise fold in the newspaper. ''It's too easy. If I know Grandfather—and believe me, I do—he's contacting every rat sniffer in northeastern Oklahoma.''

''Oh, great.'' Beth sank against the back of her chair. ''Don't you think you should have considered this before up and marrying a woman you've barely known a month?''

"Maybe."

Beth was beginning to dislike that word.

"But after dating every eligible woman in a hundred-mile radius, would it be any more believable if I suddenly up and married one of them?"

He'd dated every woman in a hundred-mile radius? Beth was beginning to dislike *him.* "That's your problem," she said, pushing her chair away from the table. "You can handle it." Her appetite had already fled the room.

"*We* can handle it."

Beth gripped the chair. "*We?* What can *I* do?"

"Go into town today. Stop at the bakery. Chat with friends. You know—talk up the marriage."

"Talk up the marriage?" *What marriage?* She gaped at him. "Why would I do that and what could I possibly talk about?"

"Everything you say is bound to get back to my grandfather. It'll go a long way to convincing him we're a very married couple. As to *what* to say—" he grinned "—you could tell 'em the usual newlywed stuff. You know, what a great lover I am."

Beth wasn't going to touch that great lover business. "I don't see why you think *anything* I'd say would get back to Joseph Wentworth. We don't exactly travel in the same circles."

"Don't underestimate my grandfather, Beth. He's lived in Freemont Springs his entire life and knows people everywhere."

Oh, for the daybed and its feather pillows. The

fluffy comforter drawn over her head. That pea could be the size of a boulder for all she cared. Just when she'd planned to spend her morning and the rest of her "married" life in a back bedroom at the Wentworth mansion, suddenly she was required to parade around Freemont Springs wearing a wedding band and a newlywed glow.

Michael relaxed against his chair and gave her another wicked grin. "And while you're talking about our, uh, *married life,*" he said, a laugh in his voice, "be sure not to undersell *me.* I've a reputation to protect, you know."

Beth didn't feel like grinning back. As a matter of fact, if she knew how to flounce from a room, she would have. She settled for sweeping by him. "It'll serve you right if I say I've had better!"

He caught her by the wrist. She halted, staring down at him. His thumb pressed firmly against her pulse point. "When it's you and me, Beth," he said, his voice quiet and deep, "there won't be any better."

Sensations, breaths, heartbeats jumbled wildly. Beth tried pulling her wits from the mass, tried finding some cool, sensible, measured response. She pulled her hand free. She rolled her eyes. She turned up her nose as if he were an arrogant annoyance instead of an arousing temptation. "I suppose Alice was right," she said, pulling some half-thought-through saying from her memory. "'She that would have eggs must endure the cackling of the hen.'"

When it's you and me, Beth, there won't be any better.

Promise? Threat? Slip of the tongue?

Beth wasn't any closer to the answer now that it was nearly dark and now that her feet and cheeks ached from the miles and smiles she'd chalked up in an effort to portray the bright, happy, entirely authentic Wentworth bride.

She stretched her stockinged toes toward the library fire. Without the energy to even mount the stairs, she'd collapsed with Mischa on the leather couch. Tummy full, he snoozed against her chest, his breath soft against her neck.

How she loved her little boy! And despite her sore toes, she'd enjoyed her afternoon in town. They'd watched the city workmen take down the Christmas decorations. Two of the men, patrons of the bakery and proud grandpas in their own right, had taken Mischa in their arms and made him cross-eyed with an ant's view of the streetlight Santas.

That was the beauty of little towns and Freemont Springs in particular. The town had carved a place for Mischa in its heart—and she had a place for Freemont Springs in hers. It was the place she'd landed, right-side up, when she'd left L.A. It was the place where she'd given birth to her son.

It was the place where she'd married.

She stared at the fire, heat rising on her cheeks as she remembered the slightly ribald jokes and hearty congratulations she'd received. According to Evelyn, Michael was home, at work in the office on the second floor, and when she renewed her energy she'd go upstairs and report on her day's success.

For some odd reason, nobody had challenged her

as even the tiniest bit counterfeit when she'd spoken of her husband and her new life as a Wentworth. Maybe because Bea and Millie had already spread the news—as quickly and lavishly as they spread whipped chocolate frosting on their famous double-dare chocolate cake. Beth doubted whether anyone she'd spoken to was a Joseph Wentworth crony, but she'd done her part.

With a sigh, she gathered Mischa in her arms. After reporting to Michael, maybe she'd skip dinner—all the better to avoid more contact with him—stretch out on the daybed and make it an early night.

Michael stared, unseeing, at the laptop computer's screen. He should be satisfied, happy even, after Beth's rundown of her day in Freemont Springs. After all, with the addition of his own marriage shoring-up—all day he'd tried acting properly sappy—his grandfather should be nothing less than convinced that Michael had married Beth for all the right reasons.

Which begged the question—what were the right reasons?

He didn't want to think about the answer.

Just as he didn't want to think about her flushed face when he'd held her wrist this morning or her almost-shy gaze just a few minutes before when she told him of the best wishes she'd received from the Freemont Springs townspeople. Mischa had started fussing, and she'd exited, leaving Michael bemused, bothered...*bored* with this damn report he was putting together for Donnolly.

Maybe he could try to decipher her breakfast-hour, cryptic comment about eggs and hens instead.

Anything to avoid facing the fact that he was married. Married!

And guilty as hell about it. And strangely exhilarated by it.

Her hands had trembled while repeating her vows. He'd gone cold then, as if suddenly splashed awake. The ceremony was a marriage, not a mischievous boy's stunt to outwit Grandfather. A marriage—to a woman whose blond hair and blue eyes had sent him sifting through the jewelry he'd inherited from his mother, his gut clenching when he'd found that perfect ring.

God. He switched off his computer and ran his hands over his face. Maybe they should call it quits before something unexpected happened. Before someone unexpectedly got hurt.

The office door shuddered with an urgent knock. Beth followed immediately, her chest heaving and that pink flush high again on her cheekbones. "Michael—"

He jumped up from his chair. "What? What is it?" he asked. "Mischa? Is the baby okay?"

She swallowed, nodded. "Mischa's fine. It's— it's—" She broke off, grabbed his hand and started dragging him from the room.

Her fingers were warm. This close, he could smell her perfume. But no. Beth wouldn't wear perfume. Her scent came from shampoo, something flowery. And then there was a crisp, more familiar note. *Ah.*

Oatmeal and peppermint soap, the stuff boxed in towers in the Wentworth bathrooms.

The stuff he lathered across his own skin every morning.

He shouldn't find a shared soap scent so arousing. So...*married.*

She pulled him to his room. The door was thrown open, as was the door to Mischa's room across the hall. She dropped his hand.

He missed her touch.

"Look!" she said, raising an arm in the direction of each open door. "Evelyn said they're gifts from your grandfather. Surprises that arrived today."

The daybed was gone from Mischa's room. Michael saw that right off. In its place, a massive toy chest and a carved and painted rocking charger—a fantasy horse that had carried him on more adventures than he could count. When Blackie had lost his charm as a rocking horse, he'd become confidante to childish secrets, compadre in revenge schemes against his big brother Jack, and finally, in preteen years, a clothes horse. With two fingers, Michael saluted the old favorite. And smiled. Mischa would love Blackie.

"You're not getting it!" his bride uttered between her teeth. She put a hand on his arm and spun him in the direction of his bedroom.

Uh-oh.

Michael smelled his sister's work here. Joseph Wentworth might order daybeds moved and toys unearthed, but only Josie would have selected the rainbow hue of negligees spread across his bed.

His bed.

His suddenly too small, that Grandfather-was-forcing-to-be-shared bed.

Michael could almost hear the old man in his mind. *You want a marriage, boy? Then you've got a marriage!*

Of course Grandfather and Josie could not know that he and Beth had never slept together. Could not know that on their wedding night the bride had slipped between the covers of the daybed in the baby's room instead of Michael slipping between *her* thighs.

Would it be bad form to count the nightgowns?

"What are we going to do about it?" Beth asked hoarsely.

There were nine.

He looked at her. Her chest was still heaving. What were they going to do about it?

Throw in the towel.

Safe. Easy. Grandfather most likely suspected it anyway.

A fake marriage. What had he been thinking?

The truth would temporarily cost him partnership in the Rocking H, but he could still provide for Beth and Mischa. He swung around, opened his mouth to tell her—

And knew she wouldn't take the money. Not after a twenty-four-hour failed marriage.

"Well? What are we going to do about it?" she asked again. Her eyes sparkled and that flush burned across her face.

Like desire burned in his blood. Like her ring burned on his finger, a sweet, wicked promise. "We're going to sleep together," he said.

5

Beth stared at Michael. "You're kidding, right?"

His eyebrows rose. "What else can we do? Tell Evelyn the newlyweds need separate beds? We might have gotten away with it for one night, but the servants will talk if we keep this up."

Beth ran her hands through her hair. No doubt it would seem *very* odd, especially following her afternoon excursion into town. Word was spreading like chicken pox at the orphanage that she and Michael were blissfully married. Add to that separate beds and—

"The stink will reach Grandfather before tomorrow's opening stock prices," Michael said, as if reading her mind.

"But this was supposed to be, um, *convenient*."

He shrugged and slipped his hands into his trouser pockets. "Is it so *inconvenient* to share a bed?"

That annoyingly casual attitude and pose of his was back. With his necktie gone and his dress shirt open at the collar, she could see the calm beat of his pulse at the hollow of his throat. He had a strong man's neck and it would be a strong man's body next to hers if she slept with him.

"C'mon, Beth," he said, the corners of his mouth quirking into a half smile. "Certainly we can share a bed without touching. We're both adults."

That's what I'm afraid of.

She was used to sharing a room with other girls. Sharing her space with her baby. Not sharing a bed with a man. Evan had never stayed the entire night with her.

Maybe that should have told her something.

"I don't snore," Michael offered.

Beth didn't doubt him. A man like Michael didn't snore. A man like Michael warmed beds and warmed hearts and shooed away that awful, cold loneli—

She'd promised not to think of that word again.

"Really, it's not a good idea, Michael." That darn eyebrow of his rose once more so she spoke faster. "I can sleep on the floor, or—"

"Not afraid, are you, Beth?"

"I'm not afraid of anything." Automatically, the response spilled out. You learned that in the orphanage. You learned never to admit you were afraid of the dark or of not having parents or of not being able to raise your little boy by yourself.

"Good then, it's all settled." He turned back toward the office.

"No!" That came out automatically, too. Orphans learned self-preservation at the cradle, as well. And some instinct told her to beware getting close to Michael.

He spun around oh-so-coolly. Oh-so-calm, his dark eyebrows moved ceilingward. "I don't bite," he said.

But what if she wanted him to? The wayward thought made her cheeks burn.

His eyes narrowed, he walked toward her. His fingertips touched cool against her face. "You *are* afraid."

Deny it! Beth's pulse doubled. Being afraid meant you could be hurt. And she wasn't going to let any man, prince or husband, close enough to hurt her ever again. She had the calluses to prevent that.

And, darn him, Michael seemed so easy with the whole idea, as if sleeping with her would be no more unsettling than sharing the covers with a tabby cat.

"Beth…" he began, and his fingers stroked her skin in a light caress. "If you don't want to—"

"Nonsense," she said briskly, ignoring the squiggly sensations tickling her skin. "I'll look forward to it."

He stilled, laughed, slowly drew his fingers away. "Me, too."

There was nothing special about Beth.

A few minutes after 11:00 p.m., Michael slouched in an overstuffed chair beside the marble fireplace in his bedroom, convincing himself of the thought. Through the closed door to the attached bathroom, he heard the sound of running water.

Beth would be brushing her teeth. Washing her face. All the things a woman did before bed—simple, ordinary.

Nothing special enough to make his muscles guitar-string taut or his blood run flood fast.

There was nothing special about Beth.

Because that was how he was going to make it through tonight. Through the entire marriage. With calm, with ease, they would play their roles for Evelyn and the household staff to convince Grandfather they were married.

To persuade the old man to resume the reins of the Oil Works.

To purchase Michael's freedom from family responsibilities.

To provide Mischa and Beth the security they deserved.

The bathroom door opened and she emerged in a thin, frayed, pink-striped robe. White flannel—a nightgown, he presumed—showed at her neck.

Nine negligees and she chose flannel and frays. *Thank God.*

She darted a nervous look his way. "Well," she said. She smiled that tight, labored smile he remembered from the night they met.

"Well," he returned. There was nothing special about Beth. No reason for him to imagine sleek skin beneath warm flannel.

"I, uh, I'm going to check on Mischa one more time," she said.

Michael didn't point out that another of Grandfather's gifts had been a state-of-the-art nursery monitor. The receiver sat on one of the bedside tables and could pick up the sound of a feather falling in the room across the hall.

A short reprieve from the scent of her soap and toothpaste and the wild imaginings of his flannel-nightgown-obsessed mind seemed like a good thing.

To make this work, to guarantee a pain-free "marriage," he had to remain as distant and controlled as possible.

She left the door to his bedroom open and the one to Mischa's open, too. From this far away, as she hovered over the crib in the dimly lit room, she seemed more like a maternal angel than a woman.

He liked thinking of her that way. Angelic instead of arousing. Haloes instead of hormones. For the first time since he spied the negligees spread across his bed, his mood lightened. He could do this. He could take his wife to bed and not touch her.

"Michael." A ghostly, but sexy whisper shivered down his spine. *"Michael."*

It took him a moment to put together the disembodied voice, the nursery monitor, the woman—think *angel*, Wentworth—across the hall.

In response to her call, he need only have approached as far as the doorway of Mischa's room. But when he arrived at that point she smiled—not her nervous smile, but that other one, the bright, warming one—and he suddenly found himself striding close enough to smell the freshness of her flannel.

"Just testing that the monitor works well," she whispered, obviously relieved. "I wanted to make sure." Into the new silence, the soughing of the baby's breaths washed through the room. One of Beth's fingertips lightly touched the baby's hair and then, as if she still couldn't bear to move away, she pulled up the blanket to the baby's shoulders.

Something caught in Michael's throat. He tried

swallowing, couldn't, coughed lightly, turning away from the crib.

"Are you okay?" she asked quietly. Her palm smoothed against his back.

Michael coughed again, straightened away from her hand to maintain a distance from her nothing-special touch. "Fine," he said shortly, ready to dash back to the relative safety of his bedroom.

Her hand stopped him again. Just two fingers on his forearm and a small nod to the rocking horse in the corner of the room. "I love the horse. What's his name?"

Michael relaxed. Come to think of it, the horse was a safe topic and Mischa's room was safer territory than across the hall. He swallowed and kept his voice low. "When he was Jack's, he was Challenger. Josie called him Beauty. Me, I went for plain and simple. Blackie."

"Was he a gift from your Grandfather?"

Michael shook his head. "From our parents, actually, to Jack. Then each of us got him in turn. Blackie made a great rodeo bronc."

Beth laughed softly. "I can picture that. How did your mother handle your antics?"

"She didn't have to. She and my father died when I was a baby."

She touched him again. Bare skin to bare skin. Her fingers against the back of his hand. "I'm sorry," she said.

He pulled away, slowly, so that he felt another long glide of her touch. "Don't be. I had my grandfather. Josie. Jack."

A silent moment.

"How do you feel about losing him?" she asked softly. "Jack, I mean."

Michael's skin turned cold. He didn't want to think about Jack. About missing Jack. Grandfather grieved enough for the entire family. "I'm mad as hell at him." The words burst out.

Michael wanted them back. Not that the words weren't true—but why talk about it? He was the expert at keeping things light and he liked it that way.

"Why are you mad at Jack?" she asked.

He'd known she would persist, he thought, annoyed. Beth was the type to make him think about stuff that was easier to live with as an unrecognizable heap in a dark corner of his mind. "I don't want to talk about it," he said coldly, stalking away from her and toward the door. "I'm going to bed."

"Me, too," Beth answered, following him.

"I want—" *Hell.* He wanted to be alone, but they were stuck in this sham of a shared wedding bed.

He shut the door behind her and instantly flicked out the light, not wanting her to see his face. In the near pitch-blackness of the room, he found the bathroom. When he came out, he could discern the slight lump Beth made under the covers of the bed. He shucked his sweatshirt and jeans and wearing only boxers, he crawled in the opposite side.

He pummeled the pillow, then flopped down on his back. Beth lay as silent and stiff as a mannequin.

His irritation with her hadn't washed down the drain with the toothpaste. And her obvious discomfort in his bed heated it to anger. "I'm not going to attack you, dammit."

"That's not what's bothering me," she said, her voice quiet. "Alice always said never to go to bed angry. And I owe you an apology, Michael."

Oh, hell. She had that all wrong, but he wasn't ready to admit it yet. "*Who* is this Alice?"

"One of the women who raised the girls at the Thurston Home. She handled most of the day-to-day care of us. She would say it wasn't my place to probe your feelings about your brother. And she'd be right. I'm sorry, Michael. How you feel is none of my business."

"You're my wife." He didn't know why he mentioned it. He didn't know why he didn't just agree with her. Welcoming his anger, nurturing it, was a much safer and distancing response.

"Temporarily your wife."

As if he needed to be reminded.

"It's just that..." Beth didn't finish.

"Go ahead." The talking was relaxing her. And he knew *he* couldn't sleep if she was board-stiff beside him.

"It's just that I've lost people, too, Michael. I may not have known my parents like you knew Jack, but I've been sad. And angry. I thought you might like to talk about it."

What he would like was to avoid the entire subject. But Michael sighed. "Oh, hell," he said. Did he feel like a heel, or what? "I'm a hotheaded jerk," he said. "I should apologize to you."

"Accepted, if you'll accept mine."

"Done."

He sighed again. "Done," he repeated.

With the anger fading, the room held only the sound of her breathing and the scent of her body. Michael closed his eyes and tried to think of the last details of his move from Wentworth Oil. Tomorrow he'd start working half days and the other half with Elijah.

The warmth from Beth's body was creeping toward his side of the bed.

There was nothing special about it.

"Do you think I'll be able to hear Mischa if he needs me?" Her breath feathered over his skin.

He swallowed. "You know I heard you just fine."

She sighed. "Yes."

In a few minutes she was asleep.

In a few hours he was still awake. Even after she got up once to nurse the baby and then fell back into bed and sleep, immediately. Her body warmth seemed to find him, no matter how many ways he turned, no matter how many times he threw off the covers.

Finally, finally, he dozed. And woke to find Beth's body heat surrounding him again. His eyes still closed, he flexed his arms and discovered them around a small, flannel-encased woman. Her rear end was pushed into his groin. He guessed that the tickle at his chin was nothing more special than Beth's duck-down hair.

He groaned softly and opened his eyes.

Suddenly, she turned over and edged out of his

arms. They were on her side of the bed, staring at each other.

The bed-poacher had been him.

The tousled and rested-looking woman was her.

"Well," she said.

He wanted to say something. Make some promise about it not happening again. Some cool, flip comment to neutralize the moment. Anything to make it nothing special to wake with her in his arms.

Her scent clung to his skin. He liked it.

She licked her lips. He liked that, too.

"We're moving out of here today," he decided suddenly.

She blinked.

"There's a ranch house on my property. The people who sold me the land left nearly everything there." He and Beth could be alone there. *Apart.*

"But your grandfather—the staff—"

"They'll think it's nothing special if we want to move out by ourselves. More convincing even." *Nothing special.*

A blush rose from the neck of the white flannel nightgown. It rimmed the edges of her ears with an irresistible pink.

Michael fisted his hands. He couldn't sleep with her again if he wanted to keep her safe from pain. Move to the ranch, he mentally urged. There, he could keep his distance.

In the bedroom she'd chosen for herself and Mischa, Beth unpacked the last of the baby clothes into the newly cleaned dresser. Her shopping bag luggage had come in handy quicker than even she'd suspected.

She and Michael had brought their few things over in the early morning. Evelyn had protested their leaving the Wentworth house, but then had smiled her understanding and done some of the packing herself.

The housekeeper had wanted to send along one of the maids to help with the cleaning of the long-deserted ranch house. Beth had said no. She'd accepted a load of cleaning supplies, though, and had spent the midmorning hours completely cleaning the small one-story, two-bedroom house. All the while really hoping to wash away her embarrassment.

It was obvious Michael had moved them to the ranch property to avoid another night with her in his bed.

It was all her fault.

For a woman who'd never spent an entire night with a man, she'd experienced the most restful sleep of her life. Michael's presence—Michael's *arms*—had brought her comfort and peace. No wonder the poor man had run scared—and with no choice but to tow her along—to the ranch.

Did he think she was getting too comfortable with him? First, she'd tried to probe into his emotions toward his brother's death, and then she'd tried to worm her way into his embrace.

Please God, make him not see it that way.

But Michael was always so calm and controlled, so ready with answers, that his sudden defection to the ranch surprised her. She knew he hadn't been considering it. She knew it had been an impulsive reaction to her night in his bed.

In his crib, Mischa protested her lack of attention. Gladly, she picked him up and rubbed her cheek against his downy head. The sweet smell and feel of him always soothed any aches in her heart.

It didn't now.

Her love for the baby rose as fiercely as ever, of course, but she still felt something—a void—that centered around Michael. Embarrassment. Guilt that she'd forced him out of his own home.

Yes, that was it.

"How are we going to make it up to him?" she asked Mischa aloud.

He stared at her solemnly.

"What if we do a little something to this house?" Though now clean, the small ranch home had the utilitarian and impersonal feel of a barracks. Maybe she wasn't truly Michael's wife, but she could expend a true effort to make the place a home for him.

It wasn't Michael's fault he'd never really seen her as a woman—except for that teasing moment in the breakfast room when he'd said things could be good between them—and she couldn't blame him for that. Obviously, she wasn't his type and she'd made him uncomfortable by cuddling close.

She'd make it up to him by adding a little comfort to the house. With a little polish and a little luck, perhaps he'd forget all about her hours in his arms.

Beth had taken her checkbook into town with her, but apparently the Freemont Springs stores had been alerted to her new status. The groceries and then the housewares she picked up at the variety store were automatically charged to the Wentworth account.

By 6:00 p.m. she had a casserole bubbling in the oven and a salad and cold beer in the fridge. Maybe it wasn't the fare of the Wentworth cook, but it was what Beth knew how to prepare. Peering in at the fragrant noodles and cheese, Beth smiled in satisfaction. She just knew he would appreciate her effort.

She'd done a little something to the small den attached to the kitchen, too. The couch there was of cracked vinyl, and she'd warmed it with a homemade quilt she'd found at the local arts and crafts consignment shop.

At the thrift store she'd found a couple of framed prints and a faded, but pretty needlepoint sampler, also framed. Hung on the walls, they added color to the mostly neutral room.

A bowl of shiny red-and-green apples served as a centerpiece on the wobbly kitchen table. Her old black-and-white TV sat in a corner of the den on a packing crate covered by a scarf. Beth smiled again. The place looked really nice.

Well, maybe a Beth Masterson kind of nice, not a Michael Wentworth kind of nice, but still, he couldn't fail to notice the effort she'd made to clean and decorate the place.

She ran her hands down her shirt, tucking it neatly into her jeans. She'd worked on herself a bit, too. Just so that Michael wouldn't think she was a total nothing. Finger-tousling gave her hair a little lift, and her face seemed brighter with the sparing use of some mascara, blush, and a light wash of lipstick.

Mischa, newly bathed too, seemed content to view the room from his infant seat on one of the kitchen counters.

The sound of gravel spray caught his attention and caught Beth's, too. Michael was home.

And not in a good mood. He took one long look at her, then grunted some sort of monosyllable to her cheerful, California-casual, "Howzitgoing?"

He didn't look at the room. He didn't sniff the smell of dinner appreciatively. He did spare a chuck under the chin for Mischa, but then disappeared down the short hallway to his bedroom.

Beth heard the shower start. She turned off the oven and set the table. He wandered back in, took another one of those long looks at her then a glance at the table set for two, and disappeared again. After grabbing a beer from the refrigerator.

Still nothing about the spit-shined house or the hot meal.

She fixed her own plate and talked to Mischa while she ate her dinner. Halfway through, Michael came in the kitchen for another beer. This time he disappeared through the front door with the rest of the six-pack.

Beth looked at Mischa. He stared back.

She heard the sound of the truck's door open and close, and the engine start up, but Michael didn't drive away.

"What could he possibly be doing?" she asked aloud.

Apparently Mischa didn't have any ideas, either.

She rinsed her plate, put the salad back in the refrigerator and the casserole back in the still-warm oven. Then, she took stock of her day and what had happened so far this evening.

"Michael," she told Mischa, who was beginning to drowse, "isn't going to sit in that truck alone."

6

Michael thought of calling Elijah. His best buddy had been a state champion placekicker in high school, and Michael needed somebody to boot his butt across town.

Beth didn't deserve marriage to a boor. Or boar. Even bore might suffice as description. He'd returned to the ranch house after a double-duty day—half spent at the Oil Works, half spent at Elijah's ranch—thinking he'd be tired enough not to respond to Beth.

Duh.

One look at her sparkling eyes and tempting mouth and he'd had to take himself and his hardening body to a cold shower. Two beers hadn't dulled the edge.

Nursing the third to the roar of the truck's heater and the twang of old George Strait wasn't doing a thing for him, either. Except remind him of how the marriage had been *his* idea and it was *she* who appeared to be paying the price of his lousy moods and uncontrollable lusting.

Because that was what it was, lust. Good, ol'-fashioned lust that made his skin itchy and his muscles—*all* his muscles—clench at the sight or scent of her. Damn, but she didn't deserve that from him.

"I'm a heel," he told the mournfully crooning George. He drained the third beer and twisted the top off the next bottle, closing his eyes. "You hear me, George? I'm a rotten, out-and-out dog of a man."

He didn't know if George heard him, but George's drummer did. He started an agreeing *rat-ta-tat-tat* that seemed to thrum right against the passenger side window.

Rat-ta-tat-tat.

George's song ended but George's drummer didn't. *Rat-ta-tat-tat.*

Michael opened one eye. *Oops.* The drummer wasn't George, but Beth, knocking on the window.

Michael straightened from his slouch, flipped the lock and pushed open the passenger side door. She hopped in, wearing her Michelin Man parka.

He instantly resolved to buy her a new coat at the earliest opportunity. But then he breathed in Beth-scent and knew that first, foremost, he had to get her warm and tempting body back to the house.

Unsure of what he was facing, he reached up to switch on the cab's overhead light. Red splashed her cheeks—from the cold, he presumed—and she was breathing hard.

He quickly offed the overhead and tried to think of something else—the single-digit temperature, the organizational chart of the Oil Works—to get his mind off her full mouth.

Looking determinedly away and out the window into the night's blackness, he inhaled and prepared a vague apology. Words to get her out of the truck. Words to get her clear away from his lusting thoughts and hungry clutches.

Maybe he'd say work was bothering him. Juggling the two jobs a headache. Anything besides the truth to explain away his rudeness and send her back to the house.

But she spoke first. "Well, I'm sorry you can't even look at me," she said.

He was so startled, that he did. "What?"

"I'm trying my best, you know."

He blinked. "Of course."

"Maybe you expected a more beautiful, polished wife—whatever. But you have me."

Did she think he was ashamed of her? "Beth. I didn't move you out here because I wished you were someone else."

The dash lights edged her profile in eerie green. "Why did you move me out here?"

He should have seen that coming. Blame it on the beers and George Strait. The *rat-ta-tat-tat* that continued echoing in his brain. "Huh?" he said to stall.

"Oh, I won't even make you say it." Disgust filled her voice. "I plastered myself against you last night. Stucco by Beth."

"Stucco by Beth?" he echoed stupidly.

"I know you don't see me that way. I've known it from the beginning. I've been a means for you, not a woman, and I understand that." She paused. "But you could have eaten the casserole!"

His stomach rumbled and he accepted it as one of

his punishments. "But what, uh, is this 'way' that I don't see you?"

A little grunting noise started up from her vicinity. Suddenly he understood the overstuffed quality of her jacket. She unzipped the garment to expose the blanket-bundled and now-fussing Mischa.

Then she performed an amazing balancing and twisting motion that he couldn't decipher in the near-darkness of the truck's interior. There was a smacking noise and then Mischa went suddenly quiet.

Michael had a bad feeling about what was happening. "Um." He cleared his throat. "Don't you want some privacy?" he asked.

She wriggled in the passenger seat and propped the elbow cradling Misha's head against her crossed knee. "What does it matter?"

"Isn't feeding, uh—" he coughed, "—nursing a baby something you'd prefer to do alone?"

"It will only take a few minutes. He's just about to nod off for his first big sleep of the night. It can't possibly bother you."

Michael didn't know what to say to that. It wasn't *bothering* him exactly. But she was bare-breasted—she had to be, right?—just inches from him and it was...bothering him a hell of a lot.

"Maybe I should go back into the house," he said.

"Not before I get my say." Beth made a quick movement and switched Mischa's direction.

Was that a glimpse of breast? Michael tried not thinking about it. January. Freezes.

"...sorry," she finished.

He swallowed quickly. "Excuse me, I didn't catch that. What?"

She let loose a long sigh. "I was mumbling. I'm not too good at this, okay?"

"Spit it out, Beth." Had she found him out? Did she want to light into him for his inconvenient hots for her?

"I'm sorry about last night," she said quickly. "I'm sorry that I, uh, kinda liked sharing a bed with you. And I know I'm not your type at all. I absolutely know it. So don't worry that I'll come on to you or anything. I'll keep everything as friendly—*only* friendly—as possible. You don't have to worry about me in any other way."

The barrage of words took a few moments to sink in. "You're not my type?"

"I know it," she said. "You've made it abundantly clear that you don't see me...well, see me as a *woman*."

The truck's cab was overheating. If shock hadn't paralyzed him, Michael would have turned off the heater. Instead he just looked at Beth, who made another little twist and wriggle. In the dimness he could see that Mischa was now...unattached and asleep.

Michael replayed her words and realized she had placed his salvation squarely in his lap. Somehow he'd given the impression that he was uninterested in her. No denial from him, and she'd do all the distancing by herself.

She'd go back into the house, leaving him the truck, the beer, and good ol' George.

They'd continue with a polite and distant marriage

and some time from now he'd simply shrug off all ties to Wentworth Oil and to her. It was everything he could have thought to ask for.

Beth lifted the sleeping baby against her shoulder. Her palm rubbed little circles against his back.

Michael pinched the bridge of his nose, where his headaches always started. If he kept silent, any minute now she'd walk back into the house, and not many months from now, straight out of his life. Simply. Without complications. In a nothing-special kind of way.

Breaking the tense silence, Mischa belched like a pool player after a sixer of ale.

Beth giggled.

And that did it for Michael.

"Ah, honey," he said. The tender mother-to-baby touch, the beery-sounding belch, the girlish laugh. "You've got it all wrong, wrong, wrong." He couldn't let Beth think she wasn't a woman in his eyes.

She stilled. Laughter evaporated. "What do I have wrong?" she whispered.

"I've been wanting you since—God, I don't know. But I brought you out here so I wouldn't touch you. Another night alone in my bed and things would have gotten out of hand. At least on my part."

"I—I don't understand."

"I didn't want you to. I didn't want you to see what you do to me, okay?" He was explaining it to himself, too.

"I don't—bother you?"

He laughed. "Oh, yeah, you bother me, Beth.

Your eyes. Your laugh. Your sexy mouth that I want to lick every time I look at it. I want to touch you, honey, and smell you, and rub myself against you until we're both so hot that January in Oklahoma feels like August in Acapulco.''

He didn't know what she'd say to that.

She said nothing. With a quick, muffled exclamation, she tucked Mischa back into her coat and jumped from the truck. Out so fast that he didn't even have the chance to catch her expression in the brief flash of the overhead light.

Michael listened to a tune from Randy Travis and one from Reba before he let himself out of the truck and into the house. As he walked inside, he added another couple of lines to his list of sins.

Lousy, lusting moods aimed at his bride-of-convenience.

Frightening bride-of-convenience with the aforementioned lousy, lusting moods.

He'd find her—probably under lock and key in her bedroom—then apologize to her, which he should have done in the first place and been silent about everything else, and finally lock *himself* in his bedroom for the duration of the marriage.

Beth was a dim shape on the couch in the darkness of the den.

Michael froze, trying to gauge what he'd done to her. Apparently she wasn't frightened enough to take refuge in her bedroom. But was she crying? Damn, he'd hate that.

Apologize, Wentworth. Apologize and then leave her alone.

"Beth?"

She drew her knees up onto the couch and he could make out that she hugged them against her chest.

"I want to—"

"Don't say any more," she whispered.

"I owe it to you," he insisted, stepping into the room. "I owe you—"

"Do you think I'm a bad mother?"

"What?" The crazy question drew him two steps closer to the couch. "You're a great mother."

She rested her forehead against her knees. "I don't think a mother should feel like this." Her voice was muffled, confused.

Michael sat on the arm of the couch. "Like what, Beth?" He wanted to touch her so bad, to comfort her. He fisted his hand against his thigh. "This is about something I've done. I need to—"

"No." She shook her head and a little wave of her scent drifted up to him. He drank it in.

Apologize, Wentworth. Apologize and then lock yourself in your room.

"I don't think a mother should..." she said, before he could form the words.

Should want to maim the man she's married to? he thought with a grimace. "Wanting you," he said. "I shouldn't have said that. I should apol—"

"I want you, too," she whispered.

His heart slammed into his gut. *"What?"*

"Maybe a mother shouldn't," she said softly.

"You'd think I would be focused on Mischa. But I look at you, and…"

She's got it wrong, Wentworth. She's vulnerable right now. "I know you said you like sharing a bed with me, Beth. But that's just about another warm body. I think you're lone—"

"Don't say it," she said vehemently. "That's not it at all."

"What are you telling me, Beth?" He tried to stop himself from touching her. But his hand reached out and stroked her soft, feathery hair.

She didn't move away. "I don't know. The truth, I guess. I can't forget that first kiss."

That was it. Michael slid down the arm of the sofa and scooped Beth up in his arms. No more talk. Her face turned his way, his face came down. His chin bumped her forehead, brushed by her nose. Her breath puffed against his cheek.

Lips finally found lips.

Her taste exploded on his tongue. He thrust it inside her hot mouth, he couldn't wait. She opened for him, opened wide her arms around him.

Stucco by Beth. Yes. He wanted her warm touch all over his skin.

He thrust his tongue into her mouth again and then hers followed more slowly back into his mouth. He sucked on her tongue. She went rigid in his arms, moaned.

His pulse was hammering in all the right places. He ran his tongue down her neck to see if her pulse beat as fast. She moaned again, and he drew her tighter against him.

Her bottom rubbed against his lap and he groaned his pleasure against her ear.

She tasted sweet everywhere. He sucked on her ears, kissed her temples, let the heat of desire dictate the next place to explore until her small hands cupped his cheeks and made him take her mouth again.

His tongue thrust, withdrew, thrust, withdrew, the action foreshadowing what he would do with that other part of his body later. Soon.

Her breasts. In the thrill of her mouth, the smooth skin of her face, he'd forgotten how much he wanted to touch them. Slowly, so not to scare her off, he trailed his fingers from her waist toward her heart. He laid his hand there, in the center, felt the *pound-pound-pound* against his palm. Burying his face in her hair, he breathed in her scent, breathed in Beth, and then moved his hand to cover one breast.

At the touch, his thighs, his knees, his shoulders—hell, his *knuckles*—went rigid. Full, lush, *lusty* breast. Beneath her shirt, her bra, the nipple was already hard and peaked.

"Michael?"

He ignored the question because desire hoarsened her voice and he knew what she was asking for. He brushed his thumb against her nipple and the breast swelled into his palm and her body arched higher, pulling away from his lap and then sinking back down against his hardness.

The room was airless.

But he let his lungs suffer and his hand found its way beneath her shirt. The skin over her ribs was hot and she lifted again off his lap as he found her bra. The fingers of his free hand trembled. But the exploring hand moved firmly, surely, to pull down the fabric of her bra and expose her hot skin and hard nipple to his touch.

Her deep sound of desire made his blood burn.

How badly, incredibly, *wholly* he wanted her made his head spin.

He pressed into her mouth with his tongue and pressed his palm against the heated center of her breast.

"Beth," he said, rubbing his thumb back and forth across her nipple. "Come to bed with me. I want you naked. I want you mine."

Her eyes opened. Even in the darkness he could see her bottom lip was wet from his latest kiss. "Michael—"

He could hear reality enter her voice. She wriggled a bit and he knew he'd pulled her from the daze of desire.

Sensations rushed crazily from his body to his brain, as if they knew there might be little time. The weight of her against the hardness of his lap. Her soft hair tickling his neck. The nipple budding against his fingers. "I want you naked in my bed," he said again, because he was afraid she would say no.

"No, Michael."

He closed his eyes. He didn't want to see her moving away. She did, and his hand fell off her breast and she climbed out of his lap.

"I'm sorry," she said.

He grit his teeth. "That was my line."

"I didn't mean to lead you somewhere—"

"I'm not blaming you."

She rubbed her hands through her hair, tousling it even more than he had. Soft, it had slipped between his fingers with erotic promise.

"We obviously have a, um, *thing* for each other," Beth finally said.

A thing.

"And I don't know exactly what is right or wrong about it. But, um, about going to bed together…"

His blood reheated at those words in her mouth. He wanted to, right now. Any instant she said. "Tell me I didn't hear that but," he said.

Her smile filled her voice. "*Bu-u-u-t,* I don't have a doctor's okay to do anything, um, *physical* yet."

"Oh."

"You know, after having a baby—"

Oh. "I get it." His brain did, anyway. Now if only the rest of his body would. He shifted on the couch, trying to get comfortable. "But can I tell my ego that otherwise…?"

"Oh, Michael." She laughed, that soft giggle she'd let out in the cab of the truck that had done him in the first time. "You can tell your ego that your kisses and your…touch are great."

His blood went on simmer again. "So the ego and I might be invited back sometime?"

"Oh, Michael," she said again. This time no giggle. He missed it. He knew what else was coming. "That wouldn't be smart, would it?" she said.

Considering how they were married only temporarily, for convenience? No.

Considering how this *thing* between them stirred up so fast, so hot?

No.

7

Keeping away from Michael could qualify Beth for Mensa. Even ten days after that night on the couch Beth knew it was the smart move. But ten days was 240 hours of sharing a small house with a man who left behind each morning his scent in the shower, hot coffee on the counter, and a hungry, backward look stamped on her memory.

And ten days equalled ten nights like this one, both of them around the rickety table in the tiny kitchen. Tea and coffee steaming from mugs.

But she was making the situation work fairly well. Make that kind-of-okay. Really, it was getting harder and harder to remember just how intelligent it was to stay away from Michael. But she had to avoid the temptation of his easy charm, his touch, at all costs. Because the opposite would cost too much.

Michael's best friend Elijah was helping. Maybe the tension was getting to Michael, too, because Elijah had showed up the past two evenings, and they'd both greeted him with desperate enthusiasm, as if his presence could single-handedly cut the tense atmosphere just as she cut the cheesecake she'd made that day.

"Chocolate?" Elijah boomed. "My favorite."

Beth spun toward him, his plate in her hand. Michael, also up from the table, turned toward her with a fistful of forks. To avoid a fork in the arm or cheesecake to his chest, Beth swung the plate away to the side. Michael did the same with the utensils. Their momentum bumped them, body to body.

Her nerve endings flared like sparklers.

The same heat glittered in Michael's eyes.

What would it hurt to touch him?

He took a deep breath and his chest expanded against her breasts.

Who would it hurt to touch him?

In answer, Mischa started fussing from the bedroom. Cheeks burning, Beth stepped around Michael and plunked Elijah's cheesecake in front of him. The walk down the hall and changing Mischa's diaper gave her enough time to recall her willpower. She had more than herself to think about. Michael didn't want family ties and that was what she and Mischa were—a family.

She just had to forget the seductive power of Michael's touch and remember the divisive power of their differences.

With Mischa in her arms, she returned to the kitchen to find the two men reminiscing over past Valentine's Day parties, apparently a Wentworth family tradition.

"Evelyn's sugar cookies," Elijah said. "And the kissing closet. Isn't that what we called it? I caught you there with *my* date when we were fifteen."

Michael laughed. "Only because you'd sent *my* girl one of those lacy, racy Valentine cards."

Beth slid into the empty chair between the two men and picked up her fork. Mischa started a half-hearted fuss that made it hard to hear the men razzing each other. She didn't mind. Holiday talk wasn't her favorite. The Thurston Home for Girls had done okay with the biggies—Thanksgiving and Christmas—but smaller holidays went by with little fuss. No egg dying or Easter Bunny. Construction paper costumes for Halloween instead of the princess gear of dress-up shoes and rhinestone tiaras that she'd dreamed were worn by litte girls in real houses with a real mommy and daddy.

"And what did you do on Valentine's Day, Beth?" Elijah pitched his voice over Mischa's snuffling. "Play spin the bottle with the boys?"

She shook her head. "I don't know how to play that game." How wide was the gulf between her and the men! They'd been sharing cookies and kisses with girls in froufrou party dresses, while she'd been sharing a room and a wardrobe with five other orphans.

Suddenly Michael leaned over and plucked the fussing baby out of her arms. Mischa quieted, entranced by the new face above his. "No spin the bottle?" he said, smiling down at the baby. "We might need to do something about that, Beth."

The tease in his voice tickled down her spine. She could almost imagine it, imagine being fifteen and her heart pounding in her throat and Michael moving closer for a kiss.

"Post office, then," Elijah said, grinning. "We played an elaborate version of it once. Stacks of valentines. The postmaster would pick one from the girl's pile and one from the boy's pile…"

Beth's imagination took over again. The Wentworth house. The wobbly heels of teenage pumps clicking against the marble hallway. Her fingers trembling as she opened the envelope with *his* handwriting on the front.

Her breathlessness made her wary. What a fantasy. She shook her head to dispel it. "Nope," she said. "No post office, either."

Elijah frowned. "You're from California, right? They got some other tradition besides cupids, kissing games and mushy valentines?"

Elijah could have no way of knowing how different her traditions had been. But it was good to remind herself of them. Of where she came from and of how far Michael was out of her league. "I grew up in a girl's group home in Los Angeles," she said. "For orphans."

Poor Elijah paled. "Oh. Uh. Sorry—"

"It's okay." Beth smiled. It was good for Michael to hear it, for her to remind herself of the gulf between them. "I don't remember celebrating Valentine's Day at all."

Beside her, Michael shifted, and one of his hard thighs pressed against hers. She scooted away a bit, and his leg followed.

"You didn't celebrate at school?" Michael was studying Mischa's face, one finger absently stroking the baby's cheek.

Beth shook her head. "We weren't in a good section of town. The orphanage was next door to a shelter for homeless families. Our classes were actually in a building on the shelter property."

Elijah grimaced. "Not exactly a party school, huh?"

Beth smiled again. "Not exactly." How she'd grown up hadn't hurt so much as it had just seemed...empty.

"Evelyn has a thing for Valentine's Day," Michael said. "Since I was a little kid, she'd start weeks before planning the party."

The gray-haired housekeeper a romantic at heart? The thought made Beth smile.

Michael was looking at her. "She'd spread out stacks of pink and red paper. Those white doilies. Glue and sequins and pens. Jack would roll his eyes and run out of the house with a football. Josie would cooperate, making card after card for her friends and her teachers."

"I remember that," Elijah said. "I'd use all those stickers and stuff. Made my mom cry every year when she opened hers."

Beth met Michael's gaze. *See? See how far apart we are?* The privileged boy who was served cookies on a silver platter and presented with valentines handmade of lace. The orphan with the downtown L.A. childhood, not empty of care, but empty of...*caring.*

They were so far apart, *see?* But the thought was hard to hold on to when his dark eyes wouldn't let hers go. When her child had fallen asleep against his wide chest. When his leg pressed firmly against hers, insisting that she see him as a man, not a past.

"No," she whispered.

He didn't blink. "No, what, honey?"

Michael's large palm cradled her son's head, and she could feel the touch herself, soothing, comforting, holding her close to him.

"I never made any valentines. Not once, do you understand?" She could feel Elijah looking at her, too, but she couldn't stop talking. Michael had to understand how little they had in common. Nothing that would rationalize even one more kiss.

His thigh was already hard against hers, but now his hand found hers, too. Under the table he laced fingers with her, gripping her hand with unhesitating strength.

"I never made valentines either, honey." Michael's voice rumbled slowly, in that Oklahoma drawl. "Well, just one every year, though I never gave it away."

Beth couldn't breathe. Michael wasn't getting it. He obviously didn't want to fight against the thing between them anymore. Why wouldn't he acknowledge how far, achingly far, they were apart?

God, men were dense.

"Don't you want to know who I made my one valentine for?" he asked softly.

She shook her head. She didn't want to know. She only wanted him to let go of her hand and then acknowledge that they had nothing in common. Nothing.

He spoke anyway. "I made a valentine for my

parents. Like you, the ones I never met and never knew.''

Michael had let her run off. Last night he'd let her take the baby from him and hightail it back to her room, like some unready filly scenting a stud.

Elijah had cocked an eyebrow. ''Gonna hurt her?''

That had made him mad. ''No!''

''You thinkin' here?''

''Don't go cowboy on me, Elijah.''

Elijah's other eyebrow had raised then, too. ''It's not cowboy to want to protect a woman.''

Michael watched the knuckles on his fists turn white. ''She has *my* name.''

''For a reason,'' Elijah had said calmly. ''Don't make it for a price.''

Michael sighed and pushed open the front door. He'd come home for lunch because remembering Elijah's words made him feel guilty and because Beth hadn't been able to even look at him this morning.

''Beth!'' He'd offer her freedom. Let her off the hook if she wanted it. Maybe he'd even insist they end the marriage now.

Nobody was home. For an instant, panic. Had she run off already? But then, no. The baby's infant carrier sat in its place in the kitchen. The basket of baby toys in a corner of the den.

On the counter a scribbled note: ''Dr. Scudder, 11:30.''

Was Beth sick? Mischa?

House to town should have taken twenty-five

minutes. Michael made it in seventeen. And found the offices of Dr. Scudder, family practitioner, closed for lunch.

Damn.

The panic rose again, then turned to anger after he called the hospital and determined neither Beth nor Mischa was a patient there. "I don't want to feel like this," he muttered. The whole point of the marriage was not to feel like this, not to feel as if he were responsible to anyone.

It was time to end the thing.

Two blocks down he found her car, but no sign of her. Two blocks more and he had to force himself not to run. Where was she? He wanted to find Beth and get the wheels moving to dissolve the marriage.

The bakery.

He walked quickly, certain she'd be there. Through the window he could see the place was busy. Apparently the month of February brought out the sweet tooth in people. An elaborately iced heart cake in the display case made him think of the conversation from the night before. Beth's childhood. No spin the bottle, no post office. No valentines.

She should have had a valentine.

And he should have his head examined. It was divorce time, not party time.

Bells on the door jangled as he went inside. His gaze ran over the customers, counterhelp. No Beth.

Double damn. He gritted his teeth. Maybe the owners, Bea and Millie, knew where to find her. He sucked in a breath, and the delicious bakery smell hit him hard, and harder hitting was the instant memory of his marriage proposal. Beth's surprised face, her damp skin, all tangled up in that bakery smell that had permeated the upstairs apartment.

No wonder the memory was so sweet.

At the bakery counter, Millie, Bea and another woman were waiting on three lines of customers. He could have called out his question, but for some odd reason he didn't want people to know he was looking for his wife.

Or maybe that he had lost track of her.

It only took two breaths before he was spotted in the bakery. Two employees of Wentworth Oil, clerks in the accounting department, passed by him with white sacks. Both paused to ask him about the ranch, his marriage, if he missed Wentworth Oil.

Fine, fine, not a bit.

The sound of his voice made Lily Baker turn around, two people ahead of him in line.

"Michael." She said it in that flirtatious way she had, with an experienced smile that said it was he she'd been waiting all day to encounter.

"Lily." He nodded. Usually Lily's wide eyes and chest-out posture made him chuckle, but today it only seemed false and forced.

She let the persons between them take her place in line and moved too close to Michael. "Having a bad day? You look grumpy."

He took a lungful of her sophisticated perfume. "I'm fine." He tried to smile and took a quick step back.

She put a hand on his forearm. Her nails were expertly shaped and painted to a high gloss. "You don't seem like the old Michael. Where's your smile? Where's the fun?''

He lifted higher the corners of his lips. "I don't know what you mean." Over her teased hairdo he watched the transactions at the counter. If only they'd move faster. He needed to talk to Beth *now*, when ending the marriage seemed so much the right thing to do.

"You *are* grumpy." Lily shook her head. "You should have known you aren't cut out for marriage. Why, they're taking bets at my bookstore on how long it'll last." She *tsked* like a clucking hen. "The Wentworth playboy and the bakery girl."

Michael stared at her.

"Just too cute," Lily said, her perfectly drawn eyebrows arching. "Just too unbelievable."

A burn started in Michael's gut. "Unbelievable how?" he said softly. "Unbelievable why?" Others in line turned to watch the exchange.

Lily stepped away from him. "Nothing, Michael," she said quickly. "I'm just playing with you."

The doorbells jangled again. From the corner of his eye Michael glimpsed a blue parka and a red scarf. *Beth and Mischa.* The relief at locating them didn't ease the burn in his belly.

"Michael?" The surprise in Beth's voice would do nothing to ease Lily's suspicions. He felt the woman's crafty eyes scrutinizing them.

The Wentworth playboy and the bakery girl. The worlds-apart dig would confirm for Beth everything she had been trying, so obviously, to tell him last night.

Damn Lily. Knowing her, and knowing this town, a comment like that would be sure to find its way back to Beth. Especially if the dissolution of their marriage followed so quickly on its heels.

Beth moved close enough to grab. He found her hand on the stroller handle. Found her gaze and held it. He tilted up her chin and pressed a soft kiss to her lower lip. It didn't taste like the wrong thing to do.

Beth's breath blew soft against his cheek before he turned toward Lily.

"I don't play around about my wife," he said. "I don't play around about my marriage."

"Michael?" Beth asked again.

He hated that question in her voice. It said she didn't know him, didn't trust him. Lily would pick up on it. He squeezed her hand. "I've been looking for you. We have a lunch date, remember?"

Bea quickly came around the counter, all certainty where Beth was all confusion. "And I promised to baby-sit." She slid the stroller out of Beth's grasp. "You two just take your time."

"We have a reservation at Oscar's," Michael said. They had no such thing, of course, but Oscar would find a table for them. He bent quickly to taste Beth's lips once more.

For Lily's benefit, of course.

"If you'll excuse us." Michael nodded to Bea, to Lily, to anyone who might doubt the strength of his marriage, and then pushed his beautiful wife out the door.

* * *

"I'm not dressed for this place," Beth hissed to Michael. She scooted her chair closer to the table, hoping the other patrons of the upscale restaurant would think she had on a skirt with her blouse instead of ancient jeans.

"No one's looking at you," he said, picking up the menu.

Beth grimaced. "Yeah, right. Just like no one was looking at me in the bakery."

His menu slapped against the white tablecloth. "Did someone say something to you?" he asked, his voice gone harsh.

She blinked. "How could they? You hustled me out of there in thirty seconds." They'd all been staring at her when she came in the door, though. And something had been going on between Lily Baker, the bookstore owner, and Michael. Her heart dipped.

He picked up the menu again, opened it almost too casually. "So, no one has said anything to you about…anything?"

What is he afraid I've been told? Was it about Lily? The woman was older than Michael but beautiful.

"Is there something you want me to know?" she asked softly. Was it Lily he wanted?

"What about you?" he replied. "Are you sick? Mischa?"

She blinked. "Sick?"

"Dr. Scudder. I went home to see you and saw your note. Did you have an appointment today?"

Beth's cheeks heated and she fingered the cold silverware. "You've never come home at lunch before.'' What had been so important that he'd interrupted his day?

The waiter showed up at their table and took their order. Then all was bustle around them: water glasses filled, breadbasket and butter delivered, their meals set before them. After a few more minutes, Beth speared a slice of chicken breast from her Caesar salad and finally made herself ask the question.

''Why did you come home early today?''

His gaze remained on his plate. ''I wanted to talk with you.''

The handle of the fork bit into her palm. She thought of the evident tension between Michael and Lily in the bakery. Did he want to confess he had a mistress? Did he want her to know that he was cheating on his convenient wife? ''About Lily?''

''*Lily?*'' His head came up and his eyes narrowed. ''*What* about Lily?''

Beth's heart bumped against her chest. ''I thought…maybe you wanted to tell me you were seeing her.''

His eyebrows snapped together. ''*Seeing* her?''

He wasn't making this easy. Beth swallowed. ''She, um, seemed pretty interested in you back there.''

''Lily?'' He laughed shortly. ''She's only interested in two things. Making trouble and Jack. And not necessarily in that order.''

Michael's voice grated at his brother's name. Beth made herself take a bite of chicken and chew. He downed the rest of his ice water in one gulp.

The instant appearance of a waiter to refill the

glass didn't dispel the edgy mood at the table. Beth put down her fork. "Is that what makes you angry at Jack?" she had to ask. "That Lily wanted him?"

Michael stared at her. "I don't get why we're talking about Lily."

Beth stared back, trying to puzzle out his mood. "Because talking to her seemed to upset you. I just thought maybe…"

His eyebrows raised. "Maybe?"

"You married me on the rebound. That it was Lily you wanted."

He groaned and ran a hand over his face. "Beth."

She didn't want to guess at what he meant by that. "Tell me, Michael."

"Damn," he said softly. "I keep messing this up."

"Tell me." She had to know.

"I don't—"

"Honesty is the best policy. Alice always said that and she's right."

Michael groaned again. "Alice, bless her ever-lovin' heart, never had a wife that should be set free."

Cold blasted over Beth's skin. Goose bumps rose at her wrists to run up her arms. "Alice never married," she said, just to prove her mouth could still move.

"It doesn't surprise me."

Beth took a sip of water to moisten her dry mouth. "What do you want, Michael? Just tell me."

He looked up. Dark eyes ringed with gold. The

wedding band on Beth's finger felt like a warming fire to her hand. She stroked the gold with her thumb.

"I wanted to set you free," he said.

Beth pressed the ring into her finger. "Because?"

"Damn Grandfather," he said between his teeth. "Damn the trust fund. Damn the Oil Works."

Beth closed her eyes. She wanted to take back what she'd said about honesty. She wanted Michael to lie to her. For some crazy reason she wanted to go on being married to him. She wanted him to want that, too. Damn their differences.

"But I won't let you go."

Beth opened her eyes.

"Not yet, anyway." Michael reached for her hand.

His grip was hard, uncompromising. She tried to keep her fingers still, but they pressed back. She should ask him why he'd changed his mind.

"We do have a bargain," she said instead.

"Right." He nodded. "We have a marriage."

Heat slid up her arm toward her heart. "Right."

"Are you sure?" His thumb painted erotic sensation over the top of her hand. "You can wait for your freedom a little longer?"

Honesty is the best policy. "I don't want to be set free," she said. Even if it would be safer.

"Not yet," he added.

"Not yet," she agreed.

"Problem is," he said out of the blue, "the ranch house is small."

She knew what he was talking about. If they continued to live together in their tiny place... She took a breath and made a decision. "Yes," she said.

He cocked an eyebrow and his hand gripped hers tighter. "Elijah can't come over every evening, you know. He won't tonight, for sure. He's ticked at me."

"Yes," she whispered. There wasn't anything else to say, really. They had always been heading toward this, no matter their denials *or* their differences.

"God, Beth." Michael's nostrils flared and she saw the thrum of his heartbeat at his throat. "It's frustrating as hell to hold you and..."

"It was my doctor's appointment today." A flush of heat waved over her face. "I'm...well."

His eyes closed. "Beth, do you mean—"

"Yes." Beth had to smile. She wanted to be happy at this moment, no matter what might come after. "Michael."

He opened his eyes, focused on her curving mouth. "I like what I see." He grinned back, and his thumb came up to stroke her lips. "We can?"

She nodded. "Dr. Scudder says I'm ready for..."

"Me." Michael said it with such certainty. But then his grin died. "Are you sure, honey?"

Of course he didn't mean was she certain the doctor was right. Of course he was asking if she was willing to go to bed with no more promises between them than a temporary marriage vow.

When she thought he wanted Lily she'd been hurt.

When she thought he wanted to end their marriage she'd been afraid.

"Yes, Michael."

8

Of course the long afternoon allowed all kinds of second thoughts. If Michael had been able to go home with her right then... But he and Elijah had a meeting at the bank that afternoon. He'd left her outside the bakery with only one kiss. Beth closed her eyes and remembered his warm hands cupping her cold cheeks, the heated taste of his mouth.

"I'll be home soon," he'd whispered in her ear.

But was it soon enough? Beth bathed Mischa in a little tub at the kitchen counter and tried to calm her wild heartbeat. With Michael around, his dark eyes following her, his touch igniting hot chills over her skin, it was easy to ignore her worries.

But once alone... "Mischa," she asked the baby. "Am I doing the right thing?"

He stared back seriously. Beth groaned. Of course she wasn't doing the right thing. Mischa was a reminder of how wrong she'd been before when it came to men.

A woman shouldn't go to a man just to fill an empty heart. "Haven't I learned anything?"

She dried the baby off and held him against her. But her heart wasn't empty. Mischa was there. Her maternal protectiveness overflowed the measly organ at the very glimpse of one of her son's smiles. Beth realized she was no longer the lonely woman who'd fatefully bumped into Mischa's father one day on campus. The lonely woman who'd driven away from L.A. with a pregnancy that only she wanted.

Lonely!

Beth put her hand over her mouth in astonishment. She'd thought the word twice without even a ripple of dread. The emotion she refused to acknowledge, that she'd always feared was…*gone.*

Mischa had banished it. She kissed the top of her son's head. "Oh, my darling—"

Michael.

The truth slid out. Not that Mischa wasn't the dearest, most precious being, but her loneliness had been a grown-up pain, a hurt that only a man could fill.

Michael.

Goose bumps waved over her body.

Panic sucked away her breath.

Despite all her experiences, all her calluses, she was in love with him.

"Oh, no." Tears pricked the corners of her eyes and she had to wipe her cheeks dry with a corner of Mischa's baby towel. "We've got to go, Mischa."

The thought energized her. They'd go someplace far away. Michael wouldn't look long, if at all. He'd find some other woman, some woman who didn't feel as fragile as glass. Some woman who didn't feel an emotion so painfully new, painfully fresh. He'd find someone who wasn't feeling love for the very first time in her life.

She ran into her bedroom, noting the time. It was well past five and Michael could be home any moment. She hurriedly dressed the drowsy Mischa and laid him in his crib. Her hands slipped on the handle of her duffel bag as she pulled it out of the closet. One of her paper shopping bags was crumpled. With desperate fingers she smoothed it out.

She packed Mischa's clothes first. Then, worried about the minutes ticking by, she pulled on her coat and grabbed the diaper bag. Who cared about her clothes when her heart was at stake?

Trembling, she slung the duffel bag over her shoulder and ran to the kitchen for her car keys. She'd throw in their things, warm up the car, go back for Mischa at the very last.

She pulled open the front door. Hit Michael, cheek to chest.

His arms closed around her.

She waited for her soul to shatter.

He laughed.

"If you were any bigger, you might have knocked me over." His hands on her shoulders, he held her away. "So anxious to see me?"

Tell him you changed your mind. He'd understand. She'd say she didn't want to go to bed with him, thanks all the same. Her mouth opened.

Nothing came out.

"You've been crying," he said.

That age-old orphan instinct kicked in. *Never let them see your pain.* "No!"

His hands tightened on her shoulders. "Did you hurt yourself? Cut a finger? Stub a toe?" His gaze ran over her. "What are you carrying?"

"Nothing." Pitiful answer.

He shut the front door behind him. Beth concentrated on a point over his left shoulder. She tried to think of how she was going to get out of the house with Mischa at nearly six in the evening on the night she'd promised to go to bed with her husband. On the night that she wanted to go to bed with him so very much.

"Beth," he said quietly. "Are you leaving me?"

She couldn't say she was. She didn't want to. She only knew she should.

"Beth, what is it?"

Mute, she shook her head. If you spoke your fears, they could gobble you up. If you closed your eyes to them and gave them no voice, then maybe, just maybe, they couldn't conquer you.

"You're afraid." He said it for her.

"Yes." The word hissed out, and she slumped, deflated. "I'm sorry, but…yes."

Unbelievably, he smiled. "You admitted that to me once before."

The memory burst into her consciousness. She hadn't remembered it until this instant. On the night she'd given birth to Mischa, she'd told Michael she was afraid. Had some instinct known then that he was the one?

He slid the duffel bag off her shoulder. It plopped to the floor. Mischa's diaper bag followed. He shrugged out of his jacket and dropped it over the getaway bags. Somehow it seemed like a sign. To get to them she'd have to get past Michael.

One of his big hands slid around the back of her head. He pulled her against his chest. "Now," he said, his voice rumbling against her cheek. "Tell me what you're afraid of."

Air stuttered into her lungs as if she'd just been sobbing. Her arms circled his waist and she held on. What could she say? "Mischa's father…" She had some vague notion of explaining how different her feelings for him had been. How shallow it was compared to what she felt for Michael. Then she'd get in her car and drive off.

"He gave up the term *father* the second he let you get away, Beth."

She nodded. Michael was right. She gathered her breath and her courage. This wasn't about Evan. This was about Michael and how dangerous he could be to her.

His knuckle stroked the underside of her chin. Feathers of sensation rushed toward her breasts. "Michael," she whispered, looking up at him.

Dark eyes ringed with gold. They got to her every time. His hand stroked her cheek and she caught a glimpse of his wedding band. She closed her eyes.

"Beth." He said her name like a sigh. He bent close and his breath blew over her mouth. "I won't hurt you, Beth. Not like he did. You'll be the one to say when it's time to call it quits."

Beth lifted her lashes. Looked into Michael's face. Dark eyes ringed with the gold of promises. She could say it wasn't time for them to go to bed. She could say now was the time for them to part. But she'd never been in love before.

She rose to tiptoes. "Make love to me," she said, and kissed him.

Michael knew he had a way with women. He appreciated them. He liked them. He treated them well and in return they'd always brought him pleasure.

Yet never before had a woman made his hands tremble.

Never before had he been so worried about getting a woman to bed.

Or been so certain it could be so good.

She'd whispered, "Make love to me," and then to make Murphy always right, Mischa had begun an insistent wail. Beth had left his arms to get Mischa settled for the night.

Michael hadn't minded. Beth would be back, he was sure of it. But when he'd first entered the house...then he had read the need for escape on her pretty, pretty face.

He would have let her go, too.

Maybe.

But instead, she'd kissed him and something hot and happy had bubbled up inside him.

"Hi," she said softly from the kitchen doorway.

Michael turned, smiled. "Hi."

"What's going on in here?"

He held up two prepared dinner plates. While desire insisted he bed her as soon as possible, instinct urged caution. "I nuked some leftovers." He grinned with wicked intent and wagged his eyebrows. "Thought I'd feed you first."

A wash of pink slid up her neck toward her brilliant eyes. He laughed, that exuberant feeling bubbling again. "Do I embarrass you?"

She pursed her lips and lowered her lashes. Performed a subtle sashay in his direction. Got close, looked up. "You turn me on," she said.

He reeled against the edge of the countertop. It was only a little dramatic exaggeration. She slayed him. One minute sweet, one minute saucy. Hell, it was going to be a night.

"I'm not hungry anymore," he said quickly.

Her eyes glinted turquoise fire. "I'm starving."

He shook his head. "You're killing me."

She smiled slowly. "Not yet."

The food was tasteless. He wasn't even sure it was warmed through. But she ate slowly, one bite of salad at a time. A dainty forkful of casserole.

He groaned. "Thank God I didn't serve peas."

Then she finished and they rinsed the dishes and she turned shy again. He liked this mood, too. He wanted to coax her back to coquette, preferably as he removed each piece of her clothing.

Finally there was nothing left to do but turn out the kitchen light. He snapped it off and she jumped. He took a step toward her. "Don't be nervous."

"Said the toothy grandma to Little Red Riding Hood."

He tapped her nose with his fingertip. "Is that who you feel like?"

He could hear her breath hitch as she drew in air.

"After that dinner? Maybe more like one of the Three Little Pigs."

He laughed. "Why do I get the feeling I'm the Big Bad Wolf?"

Her voice sounded small. "A huff and a puff and you're going to blow my house down?"

Michael tried not to sound too cocky. "Oh, honey, you've got that right."

She giggled then and he took her in his arms, laughing, too. "Come to bed, Beth. We'll have fun."

She stilled. "Is that what it is to you?"

Tread cautiously, instinct warned. "Yes." Because fun was what he believed in and what he had to offer.

A smile entered her voice. "'Kay."

And so he bent his knees and put his shoulder against her belly. In an instant he hefted her into a caveman carry. No sweeping romantic Rhett Butler thing, but just something else to laugh about when he dumped her onto the king-size mattress in his bedroom.

He followed her down immediately and nuzzled her neck, kissing her with loud smacking noises. She giggled and squirmed beneath him and made him so hard he had to lift his body away from hers.

She used the release of his weight to push him over onto his back and tickled his ribs with her little hands until he had no recourse but to bop her over the head with one of the feather pillows. She grabbed another, of course, and whacked him back. A minor pillow skirmish led to the release of several buttons of her blouse. His shirt came off completely.

Pretending he didn't notice, he challenged her to a leg-wrestle contest. The tangle of their lower limbs resulted in him popping the snap on her jeans. A second challenge caused her zipper to slip halfway down her belly. With a twist, he pinned her to the mattress, and his hands inched between her jeans and panties. In one swift movement he slid them off her.

They stared at each other, panting. The laughter died in her eyes as she seemed to realize what had happened. He was naked from the waist up. Only her panties and his jeans separated the hottest parts of their bodies.

"Michael," she said, her hands climbing his arms to his shoulders. "I've never had such fun."

He slapped on a grin, but something fun-*ny* was happening to him. Something that was making his hands tremble again as they moved to her blouse. He undid the last couple of buttons and pushed the two edges apart. With her quick breaths, her breasts rose over the top of her bra.

He put his mouth at that spot between them. He kissed her gently there and her soft, rising flesh caressed his cheeks. "Beth," he said. He tried to think of something silly to tell her, something to make her laugh, but all he could think of was his need to kiss her.

He found her mouth and opened it wide with his. She took in his tongue as if it were a taste she was hungry for and a shiver rolled down his spine. He rose over her, not breaking the kiss, to push off her shirt, to unsnap her bra and drag that away, to catch his thumbs in the elastic of her panties and push them down her legs.

An answering tremble rose in her as he cupped his hands over her breasts. She moaned, and he slid his mouth to her neck, her ear, swirled his tongue in the hollow of her neck.

Her nipples pressed hard against his palms. Her skin tasted like strawberries and mint and he was so, so hungry.

One of his hands left her breast to skim over her ribs and clutch her hip. She moaned again, and he trailed his tongue down the center of her body toward her belly.

Slowly, he let his fingers wander toward the juncture of her thighs. She flinched when he touched her soft hair. He took a long breath. "You okay, honey?" That was as fun as he could get right now.

"Michael," she whispered. Her hands pushed through his hair. "Michael, I want you."

He wanted her, too. He had to have her. All the bits and pieces, the textures that had to be his. He came between her thighs, pushed them open as he slid down to kiss her where she was soft and ready for him. She called out his name, asked for him to take her, but he had to have this first.

He tasted her again and again, his blood pumping heavily toward his groin. It was blissful torture. And then she cried out and arched in his hands and he watched as she climaxed, never so serious about making love in his life.

Mischa's cries pulled Beth out of sleep. She opened her eyes, blinked, realized she was naked and alone in Michael's bed. An instant later he came into the bedroom, wearing a pair of sweatpants and holding Mischa in his arms.

"I don't think I have what this guy's looking for," he said, smiling.

Heat rushed over Beth's cheeks. She looked around the dimly lit room. That heap by the chair might be her clothes. "I'll just get dressed and take him back—"

"Why?" The mattress dipped as Michael sat down. "Can't you feed him here?"

Another rush of heat crawled up her neck. "Well..."

He ignored her hesitation. With one hand he propped a pillow against the headboard. "What else do you need?"

She inched toward the middle of the bed and held the sheet to her neck as she sat up against the pillow. Michael handed her Mischa and the sheet fell down. She hurriedly pulled it up as she brought the snuffling baby toward her breast. Mischa quieted as soon as he began to nurse. With her free hand Beth tried to arrange the sheets and blankets for maximum modesty.

She looked up to find Michael watching her with intense interest. She blushed again. "You're staring at me!" she said, and laughed self-consciously.

He slid under the covers beside her. "I like watching you. I like making love to you." His hand stroked her cheek.

She turned her face to kiss his hand. "Thank you," she said.

He grinned. "You *know* the pleasure was all mine."

She smiled back. "Not *all* yours."

He laughed.

They sat in companionable silence for a moment. "How come Beth?" he suddenly asked.

She blinked. "How come what?"

"An Elizabeth can be a Liz, or Liza or Eliza. Lots of names. How come Beth?"

"I'm not Elizabeth. I'm just Beth. That was the name of the nurse who found me." She shrugged. "Maybe she was an Elizabeth. I don't know."

The dim light from the bedside lamp shadowed Michael's face. Stubble darkened his chin. It had erotically prickled all the places on her body he'd discovered. She couldn't decide if the memory was exciting or embarrassing.

"A nurse found you?" His hand brushed the hair off her forehead.

She relaxed into the pillow. "Mmm-hmm. I was left on the doorstep of the Masterson Hospital in L.A."

"So, Beth Masterson?"

She nodded and without thinking much about it moved Mischa to her other breast. "Voilà. Not quite like being born with a silver spoon in your mouth, huh?"

He slanted her a knowing look. "As opposed to me, you mean?"

"I guess." Did her background make him uncomfortable?

"It doesn't bother me, Beth."

He was too smart.

"We're both orphans, if it comes to that."

"That's right. But you had your grandfather, your sister Josie." She took a tiny step toward becoming a real wife to him. "And Jack, of course."

"Of course," Michael said. "Damn Jack."

They'd made love. Didn't that allow her to try to know him emotionally? "Why did you call him that?"

Michael's finger was tracing her ear. "Call who what?"

Mischa had fallen back asleep but she didn't move to take him back to bed quite yet. "Jack. You called your brother 'Damn Jack.'" Would their lovemaking open Michael's heart to her?

He slid from beneath the covers. "Let me take the baby to his crib," he said.

When he returned, he didn't turn off the light. Beth thought maybe that meant he wanted to talk, hoped it would mean that she could finally start understanding her husband.

He slid off the sweats before he came back into the bed. Her breath caught as she glimpsed his body, powerfully aroused. "You..."

"Are fascinated by *you*," he finished for her.

Air stuttered into her lungs. Heat was in his gaze. "Let's talk," she said hurriedly. Come dawn, with clothes and daylight between them, she wouldn't have the guts to probe Michael.

"Okay," he said. He came close to her and turned on his belly. His breath heated the skin of her bare shoulder. With a casual gesture he pushed the sheet to her waist. "Let's talk about your breasts."

Beth's abdomen clenched. "Michael!"

"What?"

His breath warmed the top of her left breast now. The springy texture of his hair begged her fingers to run through it. So she did.

"I was jealous of Mischa, you know."

She tried to bring the subject back around. "Well, I've been jealous of Jack."

Michael's gaze didn't leave her breasts. "Damn Jack? Why?"

She swallowed. "Because..." Michael seemed so determined not to talk about it. How could she be a wife to him if he wouldn't let her into his heart?

Michael started tracing circles around her nipple with his forefinger.

"*Michael,*" Beth said.

He shot her a hot look. "It's my turn," he said, and then moved closer to greedily take her nipple in his mouth.

The room tipped. Darkness blocked the light. Maybe she closed her eyes, maybe desire blacked out other sensations, because now she only could absorb the feel of Michael's mouth tugging on her breast, the fragrance of his hair in her nostrils, the taste of his finger as she brought one to her mouth.

He groaned—her hearing was working—and she opened her thighs and insisted he enter her—now. He grabbed for a condom and then she made him join with her. The wild pumping of her pulse matched the wild pumping of his body and she slowed him with her hands, because his hips felt so good against her palms, because her body felt so complete with his, because in deliberate slowness she could put her feelings into every movement of her body.

She didn't know if her voice worked or not, because she didn't let herself call out in case she might burden him with the truth of her love.

Sun streamed through the windows when the shriek of the phone awakened them. Her eyes popped open. Michael, his face turned toward hers, had his eyes open, too, and was looking at her as if she'd just screamed in his ear.

She took pity on him. "It's the phone," she said. "The phone's on your side of the bed."

His hand reached for it blindly. As he brought the receiver to his ear, he rolled over on his back. His arm slid around her and brought her close.

"'Lo?" he said.

A voice scratched back through the receiver. Beth turned toward the clock. It was 7:00 a.m. She and Michael and Mischa had all slept in this morning.

Michael grunted a few times and she slid toward the edge of the bed to get out and check on the baby. Michael's hand tightened on her shoulder, preventing her from moving away.

He grunted one more time, then tossed the receiver in the direction of the phone. "Hell," he said, folding his forearm over his eyes.

Beth's stomach knotted. "What is it?"

"Grandfather's going to pay us a visit."

"When?" Beth squeaked out.

"In about an hour."

9

Grandfather was making them wait. Michael shifted on the old couch in the ranch house's tiny living room. "It's a tactic, you know," he told Beth. "Arriving late puts him in the position of power."

She wore a serene mother's smile as she rocked Mischa in her arms. "Hmm."

Michael popped up from the couch. "I know it's a tactic. Hell, I've used it myself, but it still drives me nuts."

Beth didn't stop rocking. "Have you considered he's just running late? The man has been out of town for a month. I'm sure he has a lot to catch up on."

Michael stared down at her, aghast. "He's going to chew you up, darlin'. He's going to gobble you down and leave nothing behind but the scent of your shampoo."

Her smile didn't budge. She kept rocking.

Michael groaned. "You just don't get it. He's looking for a crack, the tiniest fissure. To put this marriage past him we gotta be good."

Her gaze snagged his. The turquoise of her eyes blazed in her face. "What about this marriage isn't real, Michael? What part will be pretend?"

That look and those words sent him back to the couch. *What about this marriage isn't real?* Last night, Beth in his bed, had been mind-blowing reality.

He should be grateful to Grandfather instead of grouchy. The old man's inspection would be the last hurdle to getting his trust released. Once he had the money, he wouldn't need the marriage.

Beth and Mischa could begin their new, secure life. He'd welcome back his playboy identity.

She'd find someone else to really marry.

What about this marriage isn't real?

"Damn, I hate this!" he said aloud.

Beth's eyebrows rose. "The waiting?"

"Of course, the waiting," he snapped. "What else could I mean?"

The runners of the rocking chair squeaked against the floor. "Ah. I see. You're really the Big Bad Wolf the morning after."

He smiled, he couldn't help himself. The memory of the night before was too sweet and too hot not to relive. He found himself off the couch again, kneeling at her feet. With his hands on the arms of the rocker, he stopped her movement. *"Beth."*

What to say next? Did he thank her for their lovemaking? Did he beg her to do it all over again? Did he make another promise like he had last night—that she would be the one to call it quits?

Which would be fair? Which would be right? What *could* he say when he anxiously awaited his grandfather to approve their marriage in order to end it?

"You understand why we're here, right, Beth?" His voice croaked her name.

She nodded. "One man needs to retrieve control of his company. Another man needs to be freed from it."

"Freed from family," Michael corrected. "The responsibilities." And then he made himself say it. "And so that you can have your freedom, too, Beth."

Her eyes widened. Did he imagine hurt there? But he'd never promised her forever. "Beth—"

A preemptory knock sounded on the front door. They stared at each other. Then, inhaling a deep breath, Michael stood. Beth did, too. "Stay put," she said, her face unreadable. "Let me get the door."

The first few minutes were a scramble of introductions. Grandfather, looking tired but stern, had Josie in tow. Michael groaned inwardly, unsure whether his older sister's presence would make things better or worse.

If it didn't go better, he'd find himself at Wentworth Oil Works for life and his grandfather would shortly die of a combination of grief over Jack and retirement boredom.

The old man conceded to sitting down and being served a cup of coffee. Beth and Josie wanted coffee, too. Michael, needing something to do, insisted on serving them, then joined the two women on the couch. Josie, pregnant with her first child, was talking over babies with a blank-faced Beth. Had he blown it by talking about her freedom? Grandfather sipped his coffee.

"Well," Michael said to Joseph.

The old man grunted.

Michael tried again. "Any luck in Washington?"

"I'm not here to talk about that," Joseph said.

Michael figured that meant no.

Joseph relapsed into silence.

Two could play that game. Michael ignored his grandfather and directed his attention to his sister and Beth.

Josie was talking. "And then my husband said—"

"I have three questions for you," Joseph interrupted.

Michael, mentally donning battle gear, raised his eyebrows. "And they are?"

"Not for you. Her," Joseph said, nodding at Beth.

Beth stilled for a moment, then put her hand over one of Josie's. "Pardon me," she said quietly, then turned to the older man. "I'm sorry, Mr. Wentworth. Did you ask me something? In case you didn't catch it, my name is Beth."

Josie shot Michael a look and a bemused smile.

Michael suppressed his own amusement. One point to Beth.

Joseph frowned. "How old is the baby...Beth?"

Wary, Michael slid to the edge of the couch. "Why are you bringing Mischa into this?"

Beth spoke over him. "Mischa is six weeks old," she said calmly. "And as Michael told you before, he isn't his."

Joseph crossed one leg over the other. His Ferragamo shoes, glossed high-beam bright, were as tightly laced as the old man's hands. "Who is the father?"

Beth's face flushed.

"*I'm* Mischa's father," Michael said tightly. His jaws hurt from keeping his voice level. "He isn't my child, but I'm his father. No more questions, Grandfather."

Joseph stared hard at Michael.

Michael stared back coldly. He let the old man have his way much of the time, but about this—about Beth and Mischa—*no.*

Josie, always able to reach a kinder, gentler side of their grandfather, broke into the tenseness. She redirected the conversation to babies. Some particulars about childbirthing. How to make them smile. How you held on to their slippery skin in the bathtub.

Michael found himself answering as much as Beth. He knew a lot about babies, particularly Mischa. His hand made an involuntary fist. He'd just told Grandfather that he was the baby's *father.* When Beth and Mischa left him, he'd make sure he saw plenty of the boy.

Then Beth started asking his grandfather about the sights in Washington D.C. The old man even bothered to answer.

Josie elbowed Michael gently in the ribs. "You done good, little brother. I should have come to visit sooner after your surprise marriage announcement. I like Beth."

"You're just married yourself. You can understand we wanted some privacy." Josie was also supervising the building of a new house on her husband

Max's ranch. Michael had used that as another excuse to keep her away. "Why'd Max let you out of his sight anyhow?"

"I'm picking up a few pieces of furniture that Grandfather said I could have—Grandmother's desk, among them." She looked around the shabby living room. "You could use a few things to spruce this place up, too."

Michael didn't want to tell her it was only temporary quarters for a temporary family.

Suddenly her eyes widened. "Would you look at that!"

Michael turned his head to follow her gaze. Joseph Wentworth wore a cloth diaper over the shoulder of his hand-tailored gray suit. Beth was just placing Mischa into his curving arm. The old man wasn't exactly smiling, but his face had softened.

Michael couldn't believe it. Beth was glowing with pride in her son and with friendliness toward Joseph.

Before she could step back, the old man caught her wrist. "Third question, young lady."

Michael tensed. The crafty SOB. Get her to let her guard down.

"Do you love my grandson?"

Then go for the throat.

A high whine started buzzing in Michael's ears. This was it. Sink or swim time, and not half an hour ago he'd been practically throwing Beth out by mentioning her freedom. And after the best sex of his life. Great.

Who could blame her if she took the easy way out

right now and told Joseph the marriage was all a sham?

She'd be no worse off and he'd be shackled to Wentworth Oil Works for another three years, if not forever.

Over the insect-whine Michael heard Beth's voice. "Last question?" she asked. "You promise?"

Joseph's gruff affirmative sounded. "Do you love him?" he asked again.

Michael resisted the urge to shake his head like a dog to get rid of the noise in his ears. Josie leaned forward.

Only a tinge of pink on Beth's cheeks gave away any discomfort. She looked over her shoulder and her gaze found his. Turquoise was a beautiful color. "Yes," she said. "Yes, I love Michael."

Grandfather sat back in the rocking chair.

Josie sighed and collapsed against the couch cushions.

The whine in Michael's ears flattened out and the room went suddenly quiet. His coffee cup clattered against the saucer as he set it on the table in front of the couch.

Beth returned to her seat beside Josie. In seconds they were chattering again about pregnancy and babies. Joseph was silently holding Mischa who stared up at the old man's beetly eyebrows with fascination.

Mischa looked happy. Beth's smile shone bright as sunlight as Josie exclaimed over her excitement at having a sister. "I wish Jack were here," Josie said, as she hugged Beth. "Or at least Sabrina." She sighed. "I just hope Sabrina's all right."

With those little words and that little sigh, a certainty formed rock-solid in Michael's mind. He tensed, expecting a noose to tighten around his neck. Any minute now he expected to lose all air. Because suddenly he knew.

Nobody was getting their freedom today. Or any day.

Yeah, he might be out of Wentworth Oil Works for good, but he was into a marriage for a lifetime.

Beth had said she loved him.

She'd said she loved him!

From the moment he'd met her, he'd found it hard to walk away. He could have dumped her at the emergency room, but he'd ventured into the hospital.

He could have sent her a bouquet of flowers. Instead, he'd sent himself and ended up holding her hands while she bore a child he now claimed as his.

He had thought their alliance would be temporary.

But she was at once shy and sexy and she needed him. Needed him as a father to her son. Needed him and the family he could give her in Josie, in the grandfather who would snarl one minute but then stand by her with an iron fierceness the next. Michael couldn't do less when it would be so easy to give Beth and Mischa his family.

For some strange reason he didn't even spare a thought for the weight of the responsibility.

"Michael?" Josie was talking to him. "What do you think?"

He had no idea what they were talking about. But he knew that he was married to Beth forever.

And he hoped that of all the things he could provide—security, a home, a family, warmth in bed at night—that she wouldn't notice the one thing he couldn't give.

His heart.

Beth let out a relieved sigh as Michael closed the front door. Joseph and Josie were gone.

Michael touched her shoulder. "Are you okay?" he asked. "It was tougher than I expected."

Beth shrugged. The meeting with Joseph had been tougher than Michael knew. The old man had cornered her in the kitchen before he left. "Alice always said that if you put your nose in water, you'll also wet your cheeks."

Michael grimaced. "I think I get that."

"It means I asked for it." All of it. When she agreed to marry Michael, she was agreeing to playing Michael's wife in front of his family. Who would have known, though, how much she'd *feel* like Michael's wife?

He slapped his hands together, almost too cheerful. "I think we should celebrate. I know Grandfather's satisfied."

"I wouldn't be so sure about that." Before he'd left, Joseph Wentworth had found her alone in the kitchen and offered her $500,000 on top of whatever Michael had promised, to tell him the truth about their hasty marriage.

"Why do you say that?"

Beth didn't know whether to tell him about Joseph's offer. She'd refused the bribe, of course, and assured the older man she really loved Michael.

She'd even said she wanted to remain Michael's wife forever.

She'd told the truth.

She wasn't sure she wanted to repeat that to Michael. "I—"

The doorbell rang.

Elijah stood on the other side of the door, a carton of doughnuts in his hand. "Hey, I just passed Joseph in that hulking Caddie of his. Was he—"

Michael grinned and pulled the other man into the house. "Perfect timing! We're celebrating."

Seemed that Elijah was always up for a party. He had a boombox in his truck that he carted into the house with a stack of CDs. Michael went to his truck for his favorite George Strait.

Beth made another pot of coffee and found herself munching down doughnuts and laughing at the two men. They both wore powdered-sugar mustaches and she didn't tell either one of them.

At the sound of a scrubby fiddle, Elijah grabbed her by the hand and danced her around the tiny kitchen. She bumped into the counter, the refrigerator, the little table, and then Michael's knees.

He wrapped a long arm around her waist and pulled her onto his lap. "You're having too much fun without me," he said against her ear.

She shivered.

His mouth on her skin was too much like last night. She'd almost been grateful for the visit from his family because it prevented her from thinking about the hours in his bed. Loving him, and being loved physically by him, had meshed so beautifully the night before.

The newfound feelings she had for Michael had dug deep into her soul.

Elijah collapsed into a chair at the table. "I haven't been dancing in years!"

"Yeah, right." Michael draped his hand over Beth's abdomen and his breath warmed the right side of her neck. "I happen to know you kicked up your heels until dawn on New Year's. What was that— six weeks ago?"

Elijah leaned back and crossed his booted feet at the ankle. "So then it's *you* that hasn't been dancing in years!"

Beth leaned back against Michael's chest and listened to the men banter. What if this could be her life forever? What if, sometime before Michael got the trust, he turned to her and confessed his love? Then there could be years, *forever,* with this man, this kitchen, this warm teasing. Hadn't he just claimed her son as his own?

His arm tightened around her. She looked at him. "What do you think?" he asked. "You feel like going dancing tonight?"

"I don't know. I've not been dancing much," she said. But her insides were shouting *Yes!* The more they were together, the greater the chance he would find he couldn't live without her.

"We'll get a sitter for Mischa," he said. "I bet Josie would love to spend time with him."

Beth smiled and nodded. An immediate connection had been established between herself and Michael's sister. Josie would take great care of Mischa and appreciate the chance to play mommy for an evening.

Elijah pulled another doughnut from the box. "I think you should make Joseph do it."

Michael grinned. "He probably would, if Beth asked. I swear she's got him where she wants him."

A cold finger stabbed through Beth's haze of happiness. She hadn't convinced Joseph. The man continued to suspect their marriage was a sham.

Still, Beth sensed goodness in him. He was only trying to protect his own, just as she would do for Mischa. With time she could win him over, she felt sure of it. There was no reason to burst Michael's bubble.

Michael drummed his fingers against the kitchen table. "Okay, so we have Josie to baby-sit. Where do you think we should go? The Spot?"

Elijah had a mouthful of sugary doughnut. He pointed to it, to explain his silence, but shook his head vigorously.

Michael frowned. "Okay, not The Spot. How 'bout Dangers? I heard about a new band—"

Elijah swallowed. "What are you thinking, man? Not Dangers, either. Let's go someplace a little more out of the way. You'll have more fun."

"More fun?"

"I won't even bring a date. I'll just go stag. That way we can be three hot singles looking for love."

Beth felt a whole handful of frozen fingers slap her this time. At her back, Michael tensed. "Three hot singles looking for love?"

Beth slid off Michael's lap and onto the seat of the free chair. Her skin felt cold.

"Yeah," Elijah said, looking pleased with himself. "Maybe all three of us can find somebody new tonight."

Beth brought the doughnut carton close to her. She stared at a jelly doughnut covered with sugar. It made her queasy.

Michael's voice was tight. "Why would Beth and I be looking for somebody new?"

Elijah grinned. "C'mon. This is me. Save the newlywed goo for your grandfather."

"I'm not cheating on Beth."

"Who's talking about cheating?" Elijah waved away the whole idea. "For Pete's sake, Michael, that's why I brought up getting out of the county. We'll go someplace where nobody knows us. Where nobody will know the two of you are married."

"We are married."

"What the hell's wrong with you, buddy?" Elijah's eyebrows came together. "I don't get it."

"Maybe Beth and I are going to stay married."

The statement came out low and steady. Beth's head swiveled, and she stared at Michael in astonishment.

"What?" she tried to say, but her mouth opened and nothing came out.

"What?" Elijah said it for her.

"Why shouldn't we stay married?" Michael asked the question of Elijah, but his gaze found hers. "I have what she needs. A family. I can be a father to Mischa."

Elijah spoke for her again. "But this was all just for convenience. So you could get Joseph to do what you wanted for once!"

"It *is* convenient. I'm married. I have a son. No muss, no fuss."

No love, Beth thought. He hadn't mentioned that at all.

Elijah speared a powdered-sugar hand through his hair, giving himself a premature gray streak. "But...but...you're a bachelor. You're Freemont Springs's *playboy.*"

"You're a bachelor. You be the playboy."

Elijah's gaze jumped from Michael to Beth. "You hear him? What do you say, Beth?"

I say it's everything I could ever want. How easy it would be to let those words fall from her mouth. To walk into Michael's offer and his arms and pretend for a lifetime that it would be enough.

But he hadn't said anything about love.

"I...I'm not sure what I say, Elijah."

"Beth." Michael found her hand. He touched her warmly, protectively, cradling her hand in his. "I want this."

Elijah shook his head. "I don't get this," he said. "I don't get what you're doing here, Michael."

Michael sent his friend a burning look. "Maybe it's none of your business."

"Maybe I hate to see you make a big mistake," he retorted.

Michael ignored that. "Beth," he said again, squeezing her fingers. "Don't you think it's a good idea? We do well together. You know we do."

Beth's skin burned from her wrist toward her heart. They did well together. In bed, passion exploded. She loved him.

But he didn't love her.

He wouldn't. Not if she settled for this.

"Tell me we'll stay married," Michael said.

She slid her hand from his touch. "I can't."

Michael heard the door to Mischa's bedroom shut behind Beth. He glared at Elijah. "This is all your damn fault."

Elijah snorted. "Yeah, right."

"You ruined everything."

"Then you shouldn't have brought up this great idea when I was here. You think that was just an accident? You *wanted* me to be the voice of reason."

Michael's hands fisted. "Pardon me, O Sigmund Freud, but I want you out of here. *Now.*"

Elijah rose slowly. "So you can put the pressure on her again? I told you not to hurt her, Michael."

A burn started smoldering in Michael's gut. "So this is about Beth, huh?"

"Hell, yes, this is about Beth!" Elijah shoved his chair toward the kitchen table. "You think I care about your sorry butt? She's the one who's going to be hurt, you fool. She's in love with you."

The burn flared to fire. "I *know*," Michael said.

Elijah shook his head. "Then let her go, man. Let her go to find somebody to love her back."

"I can't do that," Michael said softly. "I just can't do that."

10

Michael didn't listen to Elijah. He pushed the man out the front door and locked it behind him.

Then found out Beth had locked Mischa's door behind her. When he called to her she asked for some privacy so he slammed out of the house. Frustrated and tired, he sat in the cab of his truck for a while. At noon, he made his way to a bar where he nursed two beers while watching ESPN until 6:00 p.m.

When he walked through the front door of the ranch house, the only light came from Mischa's bedroom. He found Beth in there, a blanket thrown over her shoulder, nursing the baby. His heart started hammering against his chest. Like the night before, watching her feed her child turned him on.

His gaze moved to her face. Her expression was studiously blank, her eyes shadowed and without their normal vibrancy. A desperate urge to take her in the shelter of his arms overwhelmed him. "What's the matter, honey?" He moved toward the bed.

"Don't," she said quietly, holding out a hand. "Mischa's almost asleep."

He must look like a fool, standing in the middle of the small bedroom hungrily watching for a glimpse of her breast. But he could only retreat as far as the doorway. He slouched there, afraid to let her out of his sight.

Her shadowed eyes worried him. At the bar, he'd convinced himself that her refusal to commit to their marriage was just nervousness talking. Or some kind of new bridal reluctance. He'd believed he could make her change her mind.

She needed what he could offer. If he touched her, he knew he could bind her to him.

With exquisite tenderness, she eased off the bed and placed the baby in the crib. Michael followed her there, peering over the rails at the sleeping child. The down on Mischa's head was darkening.

He looks like me, Michael thought. It didn't seem a strange notion in the least.

Beth walked toward the bedroom door. He didn't follow. She turned down the light, but he remained at guard. Mischa slept peacefully. So had Michael at this very same age, blissfully unaware of losing his parents in a boating accident.

Had his parents stood over his crib before their deaths? Had they made promises to him they'd been unable to keep?

But Michael *could* do something for Mischa, if only Beth would agree. He found her in the kitchen. Her back to him, she sat at the table, elbows around a mug of hot tea. Steam rose and curled about her head.

Michael wanted to touch her, inhale her, bring her into his body for protection. "Beth."

She looked over her shoulder at him.

He said the first thing that came into his head. "Mischa is beautiful. You're beautiful."

"Oh, Michael." Her palms curved around the mug, as if she needed something to hold on to. Then she turned away from him.

He walked toward her, his gaze on the back of her neck. Women didn't often expose that part of their bodies. Beth's skin was pale there, the small bumps of her spine visible as she bent over the tea. Suddenly he wanted to touch her nape, cover it, keep it from being so vulnerable.

He advanced closer and as if she sensed him, she twisted out of the chair. Standing, she leaned against the table.

"What do you want, Michael?"

To touch her. He knew his touch would bind her to him.

But uneasiness was in her eyes and she pressed closer against the table. "Are you hungry?" she asked.

He shook his head. "Not after two baskets of pretzels while watching the replay of a couple of hockey games. What about you?"

She shook her head and blindly reached back to grab her mug. "I'm cold."

I could warm you. It's what we both need.

Something in his gut told him pretty words wouldn't work, though. He came a bit closer, enough to see her knuckles whiten as she tightened her grip on the mug.

He took another stride and she sidestepped toward the sink. She put her mug on the counter and quickly opened the refrigerator. He couldn't see her face anymore as she buried it among milk and juice and cartons of yogurt.

"I thought you were cold," he said. She was showing her vulnerable neck again, and the sight drew him. He walked quietly up behind her.

She straightened, whirled, slammed the refrigerator door shut. "You scared me!"

"Why?" he asked. His heart was pumping like crazy, *bam bam bam* against his chest. He didn't want to be reassuring or playful anymore. He wanted to be inside her. She couldn't get away then.

"I…I didn't see you there." She licked her bottom lip.

His groin tightened. "I'm trying to be civilized about this, Beth."

She blinked, licked her lip again.

He thought about her mouth. His tongue inside it. That other part of him in that other part of her. Hot and wet there, too.

If he touched her, he could bind her to him.

His hands found her fragile shoulders. His mouth found her mouth. She kissed him as though she found it hard to be civilized, too.

He broke away, breathing hard. Her eyes, still shadowed, had regained that turquoise light that told him she felt desire. He ran his hands down her arms. Her fingers gathered easily into his. She was still too thin.

He held her hands against his chest. "Feel that," he said over the roaring of his pulse in his ears. Did she know he'd protect her from anything, any-one…except him?

She flattened her palms against his chest. She rose on tiptoe. Her hot mouth opened over his.

Civilization fell away.

His fingers fumbled at the waistband of her jeans. He unzipped them, shoved his hand inside her pant-ies, found her heat as his tongue explored her mouth. She arched against him, moaning.

Touching her, he could bind her to him.

With his free hand he pushed up her sweater. The front clasp of her bra was stubborn, so he tore at it with his hand. Then her nipple was against his palm, hot, puckering against his skin as if it wanted a kiss, too.

Somebody moaned. It fueled him, fired his blood, made him push down her jeans and panties while she worked at his snap. Too slow, so he brushed her hands away and released his hard arousal. He found a condom in his pocket, rolled it on, then lifted her onto him, pushing into her while his body screamed in delight and his instincts shouted that she could no longer pretend she wasn't his forever.

After they climaxed, he carried her to his bedroom. Sated, satisfied that he had taken care of all the de-tails, he arranged her over his body. His palm stroked her hair, letting it tickle his skin.

His body jerked once and he startled awake from that falling-down-the-stairs dream he often experi-enced right before deep sleep. Beth moved off his chest to lie flat on her back.

Her voice was quiet, determined, a little husky. "Mischa and I will be moving out tomorrow."

Michael's insides tumbled and fell, that startling dream all over again.

Beth held her breath as Michael leaned aside to turn on the bedside light. His face was tense, hard, the skin tight around his eyes. "What?" he said.

"We're moving out tomorrow."

He shook his head. "I touched you," he said, as if that meant she couldn't leave.

She didn't disagree. Of course he'd touched her. Attraction, desire, had never been a problem between them. She shouldn't have made love to him tonight, but he'd come to her, heat in his eyes, and she'd wanted just one last taste of what he could give her.

"You and Mischa are staying here. We're staying married."

Michael was used to getting his way. That was certain. But Beth had to be as strong as he was now. She got out of bed and tried not to blush as she looked for something to put on over her nakedness. Michael's robe was on the hook in the bathroom. She wrapped it around her and then forced herself to confront him again.

"You don't want us. This entire marriage was created to release you from your responsibilities."

He waved a hand. "That was before."

Could it be possible he loved her? "Before what?"

"You and Mischa need what I can give you. Security. Josie and Grandfather. You want that."

"But you don't."

He shrugged, the light playing over his wide shoulders. "We'll stay married."

Beth wanted to scream in frustration. "Michael, didn't anybody ever tell you two watermelons can't be held under one arm?"

Michael groaned. "Not that. I'm tired. I'm edgy. Don't make me think too hard, too."

"It means you can't have it both ways. You can't want to shirk responsibility and then take it on at the same time."

He sat up quickly. "*Shirk* responsibility? Is that what you think I'm doing with Wentworth Oil Works?"

"No. Yes. I don't know." Beth moved to sit on the edge of the bed.

Michael slammed a pillow with his fist. "You don't know."

She knew she wanted to loosen his angry fist. To open his hand and kiss the feelings away. "Tell me, Michael."

"Jack died."

She swallowed at the tired note in his voice. "I know."

He released a short laugh. "Of course you do. We wouldn't be here, wouldn't have done any of this if Jack hadn't died."

A moment of silence passed and then Michael cleared his throat. "I never wanted to work at the oil company. Never. But Jack claimed it would be a good experience. Promised he'd back me when I was ready to get out."

"You didn't do it for your grandfather?"

He sighed. "Because of him, too. Grandfather and Jack both convinced me I should give it a shot."

That was Michael. Give the business a shot because someone needed to. Stay married to the woman who appeared to need that, too.

"But now?"

He stared at her. "Why shouldn't I walk away? Why not? Josie did. Jack's gone. And when he died, I realized he wasn't going to get me out of it like he promised."

"You want the ranch with Elijah."

"And Grandfather, whether he's ready to admit it or not, needs Wentworth Oil under his control."

"So we're back to need again. Michael doing what everybody needs."

"You've got that exactly wrong. I'm doing what I want to do for once. When Jack died, I realized that it was time to live *my* life."

"While still finding a way to help your grandfather," she reminded him.

Michael rolled his eyes. "Hell, you make me sound like a Boy Scout. You should talk to Elijah. He'll tell you the kind of badges I've earned."

"Why don't you tell me?"

He made an expansive gesture with one hand. "I'm Freemont Springs's favorite bachelor. Can't you guess?"

Beth flinched. Thinking about Michael with other women hurt. But she went for nonchalant. "So, you've made the rounds," she said.

Michael scrubbed his face with his hand. "Not in

the way you're thinking, Beth. We Boy Scouts aren't stupid. I've just never committed to anyone before. Never wanted to be tied down."

Beth's heart started pounding fast and furious. So, why did he want to stay married to her? What was different about now? Did he love her? Would he say it? She swallowed to ease her dry throat. "Michael—"

"But now things are different." He stared down at his hands, fisted in the bedspread. "There's Sabrina. There's you."

Beth swallowed again. "Sabrina? I thought you didn't know where she was."

He looked up. "We don't. That's it exactly. And I'm not letting you be her all over again."

"I don't understand." Beth rubbed her forehead.

"I'm not going to do to you what Jack did to Sabrina," Michael said. "He left his child and a woman who cared for him. That isn't going to happen again."

Beth's voice came out faintly. "Mischa's not yours."

Michael shook his head. "I laid claim to him today. He has my name."

Beth had to smile a bit. "Your *first* name."

Michael shrugged. "I'll adopt him."

He had so many answers. Like all the other times, Michael's confidence nearly bowled her over.

"And—" Beth reached deep inside herself to find her courage "—what about love?"

Michael's voice was neutral. "What about it?"

Beth felt her face go hot. "You don't…"

"I don't believe in it."

"No?" Beth drew her hands inside the long sleeves of Michael's robe. Her fingernails bit into her palms.

"You heard what Elijah called me. A playboy. To be honest, Beth, I've enjoyed relationships with women for a long time now. If there was such a thing as love, wouldn't I know about it?"

The question was all Michael again. Reasonable. Confident. Hard to disagree with. "But—"

"Yeah, I heard you tell Grandfather you loved me. You can call what you feel for me whatever you like."

"But I do lo—"

"You don't have to say it," he said. "It's not what I want from you."

And that was why she had to go. She scooted away from him and stood up. "But don't you understand, Michael?" she said quietly. "That's all I have to offer."

Alice's axioms kept running through Beth's head while she lay under the scratchy sheet and thin blankets at the Freemont Springs Sleep-Easy Motel.

To avoid smoke, don't fall in the fire. Too late for that to do any good. Desire for Michael had already burned her.

You can't unscramble eggs. Absolutely right. The desire had grown into love that she couldn't wish away.

Love, pain and money can't be kept secret. They soon betray themselves. That was where she'd gone wrong. When she'd told Joseph Wentworth she was in love with Michael, she'd lost him.

She rubbed her eyes and wished she could sleep instead of analyze. But she kept reliving that moment when she'd confessed her love. Michael had flinched, tensed, and now she knew that was when he decided they'd remain married.

It should have been all that she wanted. Maybe months ago she would have settled for it.

Maybe she should settle for it now.

She slipped out of the squeaky bed to peer through the metal rails of the motel-issue crib. Mischa slept, his fists by his cheeks, his mouth moving as he dreamed of suckling her breast.

He'd have other dreams. Of Little League baseball. Of rebuilding car engines. Boy stuff she didn't know about.

By leaving Michael was she denying Mischa something he needed? Something he deserved?

She thought of her own parents. Of the person— her mother? her father?—whose hands had wrapped her in a blanket so ragged that no one had bothered saving it. Of those hands placing her in a box on the doorstep of a hospital in downtown Los Angeles.

How lonely had that person been?

How lonely would she be without Michael?

The metal crib rail bit into her hand. Beth released it, stretched out her fingers, and reached into the crib for her baby. Without waking, Mischa settled against her chest. She climbed back into the bed and pulled the covers over them.

Michael didn't love her. Michael didn't believe in love.

Was that what had made it so easy for those nameless hands to abandon her? Because there was no such thing as love?

Mischa wiggled against her in his sleep. His warm heaviness over her heart made a tender, powerful pain swell from her chest. Love. It inflated her spirit like helium to a shriveled balloon.

Beth rubbed her damp cheek against Mischa's warm head. Whoever had left her at the Masterson Hospital had been wrong. Michael was wrong. Love existed. Love was worth holding out for.

Walking away from Michael had been the right thing to do. She and Mischa would find a way to make it on their own. She'd tear up that stupid prenuptial agreement and take nothing from Michael. Not when the only thing she wanted was his love.

The silence of the house was like the quiet after an explosion. Michael had been shocked and angry to find out she'd gone to bed with him tonight while her bags were in the closet, packed and ready to go. It had taken her less than fifteen minutes to leave him.

She didn't say where she was going. He'd been too ticked to ask. Now he sat on the couch in the den, listening to the darkness.

The phone rang. He lunged for the receiver on the side table. "Beth?"

"She go out dancing without you?"

Elijah.

"What do you want?" Michael asked wearily.

"Couple things. First, is our partnership off?"

Elijah knew it would take more than his plain speaking to break a friendship decades old. "You were right," Michael forced himself to say.

Elijah chuckled. "And I'm so glad I'm taping this conversation. But really, what's happened?"

"She's gone." Michael's gut clenched as he said the words.

"Well, you and I both know you're an ugly SOB, but why did she say she left?"

Because I don't love her back. He couldn't say the words out loud. "You ever been…in love, Elijah?"

"You've known me since I was seven years old, man. Have you forgotten Andrea Edwards?"

Michael pinched the bridge of his nose. "That was eighth grade."

"And I was in love with her." Elijah's voice sounded sincere.

"I've never been."

"Hell, I know that. I've known *you* for twenty years, too."

"You believe in it, then."

"Yeah," Elijah said quietly.

Michael gritted his teeth. "I want to stay married to Beth. Isn't that enough? I told her I didn't want her to be another Sabrina."

"Trying to do better than big brother Jack?"

Anger burned Michael's gut. "It's not like that!"

"Then you should be able to let go of her."

Some other emotion gnawed at his insides. "You

believe in love,'' Michael said again, just to make sure. "Why don't I?"

Elijah's sigh *whooshed* over the phone line. "I don't know, pal. Maybe because you never saw your parents together. Maybe because you never found a good woman."

"There have been lots of good women."

"The right one, then. Someone you could trust."

"Trust to do what? Or not to do what?"

"Geez, you're making this hard!" Elijah complained. "Someone you can trust who wants Michael, not Michael *Wentworth*, maybe. Or—" Elijah's voice lightened "—someone you can trust not to laugh at your stupid questions."

Michael sighed. "You said you called for a couple of reasons. What's the other one?"

"Joseph."

Michael's gut clenched again. "What? Something's happened to the old man?"

"No, no. I just got an interesting phone call from him."

Michael let out his air through his teeth. "Yeah?"

"Did Beth tell you he tried to bribe her today?"

"What?"

"Yep," Elijah said. "Offered her five hundred thousand bucks on top of what you were giving her to tell him the truth about the marriage."

Michael dropped his head back against the couch and groaned. "Oh, great. How come Joseph told you about it?"

"He was trying to pump me, too. He'd gotten nothing from Beth this morning."

Michael sighed.

"Looks like you lost it all, pal," Elijah said.

"Don't you know how to make a guy feel good?" Michael said drily. "But what makes you say that?"

"Don't you think Beth will go running to him now?" There was a sly note to Elijah's voice. "Now that she doesn't have a marriage, she might as well get the money."

11

—→ ←—

Michael knew there were worse things than becoming a recluse in a tiny, dingy ranch house in the middle of nowhere, but offhand he couldn't think of one. So three days after Beth left with Mischa, and the afternoon he received in the mail her copy of the prenuptial agreement torn into pieces, Michael decided to resume his former life.

He called Elijah. They'd meet at the Route 3 Club that night. It was Valentine's Eve instead of New Year's Eve, but this date was just as good as the other, better maybe, when it came to a playboy reclaiming the field.

Michael pulled on new jeans, a new shirt, a new pair of boots. Spit shines and knife creases weren't exactly his style, but everything else in his closet at the ranch house smelled like Beth's fresh scent.

It didn't help that he was still using her shampoo.

But he'd forget all that tonight.

Slap. His palm hit Elijah's with a resounding smack as they shook hands in greeting around 8 p.m. Club life didn't normally start hopping until later, but Michael had wanted to escape the silent house as early as possible.

"We're gonna have fun tonight," he said, forcing a grin. "Our troubles are goin' bye-bye."

Elijah looked skeptical. "Whatever you say, pal." He threw an arm in the direction of the smoky pool tables. "We have a booth over there."

Leave it to Elijah to know what a friend needed. Not only did Elijah have a booth, but on the simulated leather seats sat two beautiful women that Michael didn't know. One looked like jailbait, but he soon found out she was just a squeak over twenty-one and the little sister of an old schoolmate. When the band's lead singer stepped up to the mike, Michael danced with her first.

"Aren't you married?" the young woman, Randi, asked. She'd introduced herself just like that, "Randi, with an *i.*"

He stiffened his elbows so she couldn't step closer. "It didn't work out," he said shortly. "Can we talk about something else?"

"Sure thing." Randi, who had proudly claimed being a cheerleader at the local university, had a mouth that seemed perfect for chewing bubble gum. "Like what?"

What Mischa's doing today. How my wedding ring seems cemented to my finger.

Michael sighed. "How maybe I'm tired of dancing."

She went back to the booth willingly enough. He tried leaving Elijah, Randi and her friend there for a game of pool, but Elijah clamped a hand on his forearm and forced him to sit.

"These ladies were nice enough to agree to join us," Elijah said. "The least you can do is be sociable."

Sociable. God, he'd always been a sociable man. The golden, glowing younger son of the Wentworth family. Skating the surface of relationships. Never even close to putting a ring on a woman's finger. Always walking away before things got too serious.

This time, he knew that being left behind was hell.

He took a long pull at his draft beer. The women started chattering, comparing the looks of the band's drummer to actor Val Kilmer. Michael tried imagining either one of them pregnant, alone, driving across country and then supporting herself at the bakery. Not fair, he thought. No one was Beth.

To divert the direction of his mind, he turned toward Elijah and slammed down his mug. "Enough of my hiding out. I'm coming over tomorrow and we'll get going on our plans for expansion of the ranch. Don't we have another meeting with that banker next week?"

Elijah's eyebrows rose over his own frosty glass. He swallowed. "I thought you told me Beth tore up your prenup."

"Yeah." Michael ignored a quick stab. "So what?"

"So I told you this a few days ago. Joseph was trying to get her to spill about your fake marriage."

Michael heard the echo of Beth's voice. *What about this marriage isn't real?* "Yeah, yeah, yeah. So what?"

Elijah waved his hand in front of Michael's face. "Hello in there. Don't you think this means she's told Joseph? Spilled the beans? As in, see you later all that pretty money your grandfather was going to release to you?"

Michael blinked. He'd heard what Elijah had said the other night about Joseph's bribe, but it hadn't sunk in. He'd been reeling from the ego blow of losing Beth. "What are you getting at?" he said slowly.

Elijah slid a sidelong look toward the two women in their booth, still caught up in their own conversation. "That Beth sold you out."

Michael laughed.

Elijah raised his brows. "Don't fool yourself, Michael. You chose to marry her because she needed the security, the *money* you offered. Why wouldn't she go for the main chance?"

Michael laughed again. "You don't get it at all. Get *her* at all."

Elijah sat back and crossed his arms over his chest. "So, tell me."

"She made me feel protective as hell from the first moment I met her," he said. "I don't know if it was that ratty coat of hers, or what."

He remembered her delivering her baby, her hands wrapped around his. "And for some reason I felt responsible for her, and Mischa too, almost instantly."

And then he thought of her in his bed, her pale skin gleaming, her pale hair mussed by his hands. "And, God, I lust after her."

"What does that have to do with the price of potatoes and Beth accepting Joseph's bribe?" Elijah said drily.

"I'm telling you I know her," Michael said flatly. "She wouldn't do it, Elijah. I know Beth. And I trust her."

The last four words fell into a well of silence.

Then the words swam around in Michael's mind, bumping into the others he'd just told Elijah. Protectiveness, responsibility, lust.

Trust.

The two women were looking at him, including Randi with an *i,* her cheerleader-smile fixed on her face. He imagined her perched on the top of a human pyramid. Give me a *P.* Give me an *R.* Give me an *L.* Give me a *T.* What's that spell?

Protectiveness. Responsibility. Lust. Trust.

What did that spell?

Love.

Well, he'd always been a lousy speller. And obviously slow at realizing some other stuff, too. He hadn't recognized what his wanting of Beth was. Or, when she was gone, what the urge to drink beers and listen to George Strait at his most melancholy meant.

"I'm in love with her, Elijah," he said.

The other man was grinning. "I knew you'd figure it out."

* * *

Evelyn met Michael at the door of his grandfather's house. While technically she should be off duty at this time of the evening, he wasn't surprised to see her and she didn't seem surprised to see him.

"Mr. Wentworth is upstairs in his office," she said.

Michael climbed the staircase, his steps muffled by the plush runner. But his grandfather would expect him anyway. Evelyn would buzz him with news of the visitor from her own office off the kitchen.

He knocked on the paneled office door.

"Come in, Michael."

Michael smiled to himself. He never crossed this threshold without a little I-didn't-mean-to-bash-the-fender nervousness. But it was time to confront his grandfather man to man.

The old guy looked as stern as ever across the polished expanse of his desk. Michael shook his head ruefully. "That frown almost makes my knees quake."

Joseph snorted. "Almost?" he asked in a near roar. "I must be losing my touch."

Michael shook his head again. "Nah. Never that, Grandfather."

With his foot, he hooked the leg of the nearby chair and dragged it closer to his grandfather's desk. The leather seat squealed as he sat down. No wonder this room engendered memories of pain.

He took a breath. "I don't want to work at Wentworth Oil Works, Grandfather. I married to weasel out of it, but that was—''

"A boy's trick."

He had been going to say cowardly, but a boy's trick sounded a lot better. And maybe more of the truth.

"I want you in the business, son."

"Yeah, I know you do, Grandfather—"

"And with Jack gone, who—"

"You, Grandfather. You and then the next person you find who loves the business like you do."

"But with Jack—"

Michael slammed his hand on the arm of the chair. "But with Jack, nothing! This is about me and *my* life! I've been mad as hell at him for dying, but now I think I can let that part go." He found himself on his feet, pacing around his grandfather's office. "Because at least Jack's death taught me something. Better not wait around for the right time to start living!"

And what he'd been doing before this was just playing. At work. At women. Even after Jack died, he'd been so determined to avoid his own problems, and feelings, that he hadn't recognized what he'd felt for Beth was love.

"So, you think you've grown up, then?" his grandfather asked gruffly.

Michael thought of his commitment to Elijah and their ranch. The depth of his feelings for Mischa and Beth. "Marriage will do that to a guy," he said quietly.

"Maybe it will," his grandfather agreed. His

mouth didn't smile, of course, but Michael swore he saw one all the same.

So, how do you find a runaway wife?

You start with the place you found her. That was technically his grandfather's house, but Michael figured the bakery was the most logical place to start. Beth had been with Bea and Millie before their marriage and might have gone back to them once she'd left it.

Of course, Valentine's Day was the big time in the bakery business. Through the plate glass window, Michael couldn't even see either of the proprietors over the crowd of customers.

Inside the store was not any different. *Hell,* Michael thought, *I won't even be able to get close enough to shout a question at Bea or Millie.* Just as he prepared to back out of the shop, the sea of people parted for a large valentine cake with the frosted message: To Little Bill, from your eversmoochin' Big Mama. Behind the cake, holding the edges of the untopped box, was a woman about four feet high.

Michael nearly swallowed his tongue. *The mouse nurse!*

To avoid meeting her eyes, he scanned over the crowd. There was another movement in the wall of people, and then he saw her. The most beautiful sight. Blond hair, sweet smile. *Beth.*

The wall reclosed. Michael drew in a fast breath. What to do? Pole-vaulting over the crowd seemed out of the question. Shouting to her across the customers equally ridiculous.

Customers. That way he'd be assured a few moments of her time. Michael hastily pulled a slip of paper from the tongue of a number-dispenser. Eighty-eight.

"Number twenty-six!" he heard Beth call from the direction of the counter.

Michael groaned.

An overcoated man slanted him a sympathetic look. "I'm sixty-two," he said.

Michael grimaced, not sure if that was the guy's age or the number on his slip. Either way, they'd both be ready for retirement by the time they were called.

Somebody crowded behind Michael to get to the number dispenser. He stepped away, knocking into the Kiwanis Club's candy machine. A lady shrieked as it tipped her way. Michael pulled the damn thing into his arms before it wreaked any damage. The lady stared at him frostily.

Michael smiled at her. "What number slip do you have?" he asked politely.

"Thirty," she said through her nose.

Michael grabbed for his wallet. "I'll give you fifty bucks for it."

"You won't," she responded, shocked.

A teenager with a puce T-shirt and an earring turned toward him. "I have twenty-seven."

Michael held out a hundred-dollar bill. The kid snatched it and dashed out the door, maybe worried that Michael would change his mind.

No way, he thought. *I'm getting you back, Beth.*

"Number twenty-seven!" Michael pushed his way toward the counter to face—

Bea.

She beamed. "What can I do for you today, Michael?"

Standing to her side, helping another customer—lucky number twenty-six—was his wife.

"I'm here to talk to Beth," he said.

She looked at him, then looked at Bea and shook her head frantically.

"If you want something, I'll be the one to help you, Michael," Bea said firmly.

Michael planted his feet. "That's fine. I'd like my wife and my son back."

Beth blushed as she wound twine around a pink box for customer twenty-six. Bea frowned. "Some *baked goods,* young man."

"I just want to talk to her, Bea. And where's Mischa?"

Bea softened. "Right over there, sleeping like a lamb."

Through a glass case two trays deep with frosted heart cookies he could see Mischa, snoozing in his stroller. One wheel of the contraption still listed, giving the little boy a slightly rakish look.

Michael's heart twisted like a horse's tail in the breeze. *My son.*

He looked over at Beth. "I was an idiot, okay? Come back to me."

She shook her head. "Not now, Michael." The customer she was helping started speaking to her.

"Then when?" he said. "When?"

Bea harrumphed. "Did you want some baked goods or not?"

Michael ran his hand through his hair. "A pie—no, a cake. With an inscription."

"Those must be ordered twenty-four hours in advance." Bea appeared delighted to tell him the news.

Michael spoke through clenched teeth. "Give me a break here, will you? Don't you like happy endings?"

Bea smiled primly. "As long as you work for them." Her expression eased. "What do you want the cake to say, Michael? I'm sure I can convince Millie to do it up for you quick."

He thought fast. "For Beth. Maybe it started out as something convenient. Maybe I didn't know anything about being a husband or father, but—"

"Wait!" Bea was laughing. "I think our biggest sheet cake is twenty inches by fourteen. We can fit 'Beth' and the stuff about you knowing dog doo about being a husband. Do you want roses or confetti on that?"

Michael wanted to hold his head in his hands. None of this was going right. Roses or confetti? He wanted his wife in his arms and his son in a stroller with a wheel he should have repaired weeks ago.

"Have pity on me, Bea."

"Michael." Beth's voice.

He turned quickly, hoping it was all going to be right. "Yes?"

She gestured over the counter to the woman beside him, customer twenty-six. Beneath her unbuttoned overcoat he could see hospital scrubs. Storks on them. A compadre of the mouse.

"This is Jenny Campbell," she said.

Michael blinked. Introductions at a time like this?

"She was my Lamaze instructor," Beth added.

Yeah? Michael looked hard at Beth and noticed something new, a sheen of excitement in her eyes.

"My *Lamaze* instructor," she said again.

Lamaze.

Beth nodded at him. "And she just told me an old pal of mine has been admitted to the hospital in labor."

It took Michael's mind a moment to catch up. And then he got it. Sabrina. In labor. He grabbed Beth's hand, ready to pull her over or under the counter, whatever it took. "You gotta come with me."

He looked over at Bea, grinning. "And we'll need another cake," he said. "This one needs to say 'Welcome to the world, Baby Wentworth!'"

Beth's hands were clammy on the steering wheel of her car. Michael sat in the passenger seat beside her, fiddling with the heater controls. Mischa lay quietly in his car seat, the entire reason they'd taken her vehicle instead of Michael's truck.

Of course she should have stayed at the bakery. But Michael's hand on hers, his excitment over finding Sabrina was infectious. Before leaving Bea and Millie's, he'd reached his grandfather and Josie, who was still in town. They planned to rendezvous at the hospital.

A tepid blast of warmth coughed through the heater vents. Michael swore. "You need a new car. You need a new coat. You've got to let me fix Mischa's stroller. Or, heck, we'll get a new one."

Beth's heart jumped into her throat. Michael the rescuer again. This is who she had to resist. "We're fine with what we have," she said.

He ran a hand through his hair. It sprang back over his forehead and she remembered how it felt against her hands. How she stroked it when she drew him against her breast. Goose bumps went crazy over her skin.

"Look!" He pointed to the small amount of flesh between her ears and the collar of her parka. "You're freezing." He put his hand on her thigh and rubbed briskly.

Beth gulped a deep breath. Only Michael had ever looked at her so closely—to see chills on four square inches of skin—or cared for her so sweetly. But he didn't love her. She had to hold out for love.

His palm still rubbed her jeaned thigh. Oh, but he could warm her and it would be so easy to succumb.

In the hospital parking lot she braked the car, but didn't turn off the ignition. "I don't belong here," she said, not looking at him. "I'll go back to the bakery. You can get a ride, can't you?"

He reached over and twisted the key. "You belong with me."

She had to look at him then. She had to notice he still wore his wedding band—she still wore hers, too—and that his dark eyes still had that transfixing, mesmerizing band of gold around their edges.

Her hands started to tremble, and she gripped the steering wheel to hide the movement. "Michael, we've been through this already."

He shoved both hands through his hair. "Damn. I thought we could do this later. After we checked on Sabrina."

"Do what?"

Mischa started whimpering. Beth moved, but Michael put his hand on her arm. "Let me," he said. "He's probably just cold."

Twisting in his seat, he plucked Mischa out of his car seat. He brought them nose to nose. "Hey, little guy," he said, smiling. Then he drew the infant inside his overcoat so that only the baby's eyes and nose peeked out between the buttons.

Beth thought her heart would break.

Little League. Car engines. Boy stuff.

But she couldn't return to Michael for the wrong reasons.

He must have seen the pain on her face, because he reached out and chucked her under the chin. "I'm sorry I've made you unhappy."

"'Leave a log in the water as long as you like. It will never be an alligator,'" she murmured.

Michael's jaw tightened. "You know, I'm beginning to thoroughly dislike this old-world wisdom of yours. What's that supposed to mean?"

She shrugged. "That I shouldn't have expected you to become something you're not."

He breathed in sharply. "The playboy can't become a husband and father."

She nodded.

He took another quick breath. "And what if the playboy grows up? What if he knows he's been skating the surface of life but now realizes he better start living it instead?"

Mischa was staring at her with the same serious intensity as Michael. Beth's heart lurched.

Michael's voice was hoarse. "What if the playboy's brother died at thirty-five and then he witnessed a baby being born and at the same time found a woman who had courage, beauty and strength? Wouldn't that change him?"

Beth swallowed. Her voice was hoarse, too, when she spoke. "It would change him. Of course, it would. But he still might not believe in love."

"Because he'd never experienced it." Michael snatched her hand from her lap and held it between his hard, warm palms. "Beth, I've been an idiot. All the things I felt...all the things you make me feel...I didn't know—"

He broke off and pressed their linked hands to his chest, as if he could communicate all that was in him directly into her body.

His heart pumped heavily against her fingers. But she had to have the words. She had to hear them to know.

"Michael?"

His heart quickened beneath her fingers. His

hands pressed harder against hers. "I love you, Beth. Before, I didn't know what to call it, this mishmash of feelings, but you've got to believe me. Nothing less could make me feel this miserable without you."

Beth's heart started pounding in time with his. "You have devious ways of getting what you want," she said. It couldn't be. He couldn't really love her.

One of his hands drifted over her hair. "C'mon, honey. Can't you believe someone would want you? Because I do so very, very much."

Someone wanted her? Michael? Maybe that *was* hard to believe. Beth Masterson, named for the nurse who had found her abandoned on the Masterson Hospital doorstep could be wanted, really wanted, *loved* by someone?

It was what she'd searched for her entire life.

And here it was, like a shiny toy that just *couldn't* be meant for her.

If you want something more than anything, be prepared to stake everything. Alice had said that, too. And this beautiful man beside her, the one cradling her son, she wanted more than toys, and Halloween costumes and valentines.

"If I give you my love..." If she gave her everything, what would he return? New cars, new coats, something brand-spanking-new as if that would make her happy?

"You'll have mine back ten-fold," he said.

Her stomach fell. Tears burned the corners of her eyes. But she smiled. "You do love me."

His face was serious. "Oh, God, I do." Then he grinned joyously and leaned toward her for a quick, bruising kiss. "Poof! The log becomes the alligator." His grin widened. "Hey, a whole new take on the frog and the prince."

Beth laughed, then cried, then dried her tears on Michael's shoulder as he took her in his arms. When Mischa protested his role as the peanut butter in the parent sandwich, they broke apart and headed into the hospital. Other important business was happening today.

Arms wrapped around each other, they hurried into the maternity reception area. Joseph Wentworth was there and Josie, glowing like a birthday candle.

Beth smiled at both of them. Her family.

She turned to Michael, who was holding Mischa. Her men.

Her husband slanted her a glance. "I like the smile," he said.

"I love you," she answered.

A click and a flash accompanied Michael's kiss, though it was lost to Beth in the burst of passion between them.

But the moment made a nice photograph in the next edition of the *Freemont Springs Daily Post.* Valentine's Day had meant lots of exciting doings for the Wentworth family.

People throughout the town sighed over the love shining from former playboy Michael Wentworth for his new bride Beth.

Bea and Millie thrilled to the happy ending for the young woman they had taken under their wing.

Dr. Mercer Manning, D.D.S., closely inspected the gleaming gums of Michael and Beth's baby boy smiling for the camera. And to think, yet another Wentworth infant—Jack's—had been born that day! Dr. Manning rubbed his hands together and smiled to himself. Ah. Another generation of dental work.

Life was grand.

*   *   *   *   *

FOLLOW THAT BABY
*into Silhouette Intimate Moments
in February 1999, when* USA Today
*bestselling author Merline Lovelace draws
the series to its exciting conclusion with*
THE MERCENARY AND THE NEW MOM.

Turn the page
for a sneak preview of the final
FOLLOW THAT BABY title,

THE MERCENARY AND THE NEW MOM

by *USA Today* bestselling author
Merline Lovelace,

available in
Silhouette Intimate Moments
in February 1999....

Sabrina Jensen would never know what pulled her from a light doze that cold, foggy March afternoon.

It could have been the heightened instincts of a new mom, still on constant red alert to the slightest sound from the newborn napping in the hooded white wicker bassinet.

It could have been the sense of danger that had dogged Sabrina day and night for the past several months. The danger that had kept her on the run, alone and pregnant and increasingly desperate, until finally she'd been forced to accept help from the family of the man she'd loved and lost so many months ago...the same family she'd believed wanted to take her baby from her.

Whatever woke her, Sabrina's gaze went instantly to the bassinet she'd rolled into the toasty-warm living room of the luxurious guest cottage.

Still nervous, still frightened for her baby even here, on the heavily guarded grounds of the Wentworth estate, she'd wanted her three-week-old infant near her while she tried to absorb the intricacies of *Advanced Marketing Statistics.*

When Sabrina saw the bassinet's snowy-white outline in the dim shadows and heard no fretful sounds from the infant tucked inside, the fear gripping her heart eased. She was safe here. At last, she'd found sanctuary. Tomorrow, her baby would be christened. Everyone was coming tonight for dinner, and would stay over for the ceremony.

Everyone except the baby's father.

Aching with the constant sense of loss she carried tucked just under her heart, Sabrina felt the need to touch her baby. To brush a finger against the sleeping child's feather-soft cheek. Tossing aside a fleecy orange-and-black Oklahoma State University throw, she started to push herself off the leather sofa placed to catch both light and warmth from the fire in the stone fireplace. Her statistics textbook tumbled off her lap and hit the colorful, braided rag rug with a thud.

The noise caused a small movement in the shadows. The stir was so slight, so instantly stilled, that Sabrina almost missed it. She blinked once more to clear the last of the sleepy haze from her eyes. This time, her gaze penetrated the gloom beyond the heirloom wicker basket that held her baby.

Shock froze her where she sat. Her chest squeezed. She felt a single instant of piercing joy.

"Jack!"

At her strangled gasp, the gaunt, bearded figure

in the shadows turned his head. Slowly, so slowly, his mouth twisted into a travesty of the smile that had melted her bones the first time she saw it.

"Well, well. Sleeping Beauty wakes."

It was the Oklahoma drawl she remembered all too well. Husky. Masculine. As soft and as tough as rainwater on rawhide.

"And without a kiss from her prince," he added in a low growl.

His words evoked a memory that sent sharp, stinging hurt piercing through every inch of her skin. The pain needled right through the terror that was rushing in to replace her brief, soaring instant joy. He'd said those same words to her before, the day they'd met. The agony of hearing them again after so many months of heartache almost tore her apart.

Even greater than her agony, however, was her fear for her baby. Her whole body shaking, Sabrina finally pushed herself off the couch and faced the man she'd tumbled headlong into love with a short lifetime ago.

"You don't..." Her throat tight and aching, she forced out the same response she'd given him then. "You don't look much like a prince."

"I guess we've both learned that appearances can be deceiving."

A sudden wave of terror gripped her as Jack stepped around the bassinet and into the light. With his skin stretched taut across his cheekbones and his face stubbled with a rough, straggly beard, he looked as though he'd traveled to hell and back.

He had! She saw it in his eyes. Heard it in his voice.

Oh, God! How could she ache for him? How could she want to throw herself into his arms and at the same time feel her fingers curling into claws at the thought of his hands on her body? How could he raise a flood of heat in her belly with that twisted smile, even as she furtively searched the shadowy living room for her purse with its concealed handgun?

As if sensing her rising panic, he halted a few steps away. The firelight glinted on his tobacco brown hair, once so short and neat, despite its stubborn tendency to curl when Sabrina ran her fingers through it.

Desperately, she inched sideways. Away from the bassinet. Toward the gun she'd bought after the first attempt on her life.

"They said…" She wet her lips. In a ragged whisper, she begged him to understand what she'd done. What she had to do to protect her child. "They said you died when that offshore rig blew up."

The look in his eyes was so cruel Sabrina felt its slice where she stood. "There were times I wished I had."

A million questions consumed her, but the months of fear she'd lived with, the desperation she'd experienced, winnowed them down to just a few.

"How could you?" She fought to drag breath into her aching lungs. "How could you go off like that? How could you rush off to fight a battle that wasn't your own, like...like some damned mercenary when I...when we...?''

"I came back, Sabrina." A muscle worked in the side of his face. "I promised you I would...."

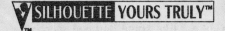
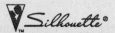

Take 2 bestselling love stories FREE

Plus get a FREE surprise gift!

Special Limited-Time Offer

Mail to Silhouette Reader Service™

3010 Walden Avenue
P.O. Box 1867
Buffalo, N.Y. 14269-1867

YES! Please send me 2 free Silhouette Yours Truly™ novels and my free surprise gift. Then send me 4 brand-new novels every other month, which I will receive months before they appear in bookstores. Bill me at the low price of $2.90 each plus 25¢ delivery and applicable sales tax, if any.* That's the complete price, and a saving of over 10% off the cover prices—quite a bargain! I understand that accepting the books and gift places me under no obligation ever to buy any books. I can always return a shipment and cancel at any time. Even if I never buy another book from Silhouette, the 2 free books and the surprise gift are mine to keep forever.

201 SEN CH72

Name	(PLEASE PRINT)
Address	Apt. No.
City	State	Zip

This offer is limited to one order per household and not valid to present Silhouette Yours Truly™ subscribers. *Terms and prices are subject to change without notice. Sales tax applicable in N.Y.

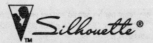

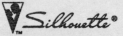

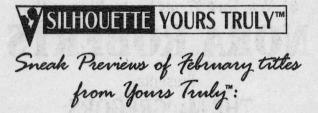

Sneak Previews of February titles from Yours Truly™:

WEDDING? IMPOSSIBLE!
Weddings, Inc.
by Karen Templeton

Zoe needed one thing to make her life perfectly peaceful—to get her matchmaking mother to stop pushing her down the aisle! So in exasperation, Zoe agreed to the blind date her family had set up. She figured this might be the perfect thing to get her mind off her gorgeous, available—but antimarriage—business nemesis, Mike. She was all set to meet her mystery man—until she started to find out more about him. Like he was gorgeous, available…and had a business nemesis named Zoe....

BACHELORETTE BLUES
by Robyn Amos

The chain letter promising true love was a joke…right? Shayna Gunther already had her true love picked out—in fact, she had three of them on her list of potential Mr. Rights. Just because her well-ordered life had turned upside down when she threw the letter away didn't mean a thing. But when sexy Max Winston showed up, maybe it was time for Shayna to rethink her Mr. Right list—and start searching her apartment for that letter!